Part One

Sarah

Milk runs in a steady stream from Zach's overflowing bowl to the lip of the table and then to the floor, where it pools on the Italian marble tiles. Sarah is entranced for a moment by the vivid shock of white against dark brown tile, thinking—absurdly—*chocolate milk.* By the time she has grabbed the roll of paper towels and knelt to mop up the mess, the dog has discovered it and is lapping delightedly at the milk puddle, sending sprays of white in every direction.

"Mama, you know what?" Zachary is bent over his bowl, studying Rice Krispies with the intensity of a chemist in the laboratory. "Snap, Crackle and Pop are really the same exact noises!! They have different names but they make the same sound. Listen. Mama, listen!"

Sarah finishes cleaning the floor and pours her second cup of coffee. Her son will be a brilliant scientist someday. She will promise him that he can do anything he wants to do—fly to Jupiter or find a cure for AIDS—even if it's not true. Never mind the million obstacles he will never see coming. Those are the little lies a parent tells, she thinks as she puts the milk carton away in the fridge and reaches for the maple syrup. Otherwise, no kid would ever get up out of bed in the morning and go to school.

This morning things are getting away from her earlier than usual. Pancakes, Zach's favorite, have turned out to be a spectacular flop. Somehow the smell of the pancakes cooking is making Zach scream. Well, it's probably not the pancakes themselves, Sarah realizes, but the butter that burned in the skillet while she was getting paper towels and blotting up milk. "It's a really, REALLY bad smell!!" her son wails, both hands clamped over his nose as if his life depends upon keeping out any trace of the offending odor.

Zach is what child development experts call politely a "challenging" child. His sensory receptors are stuck in permanent overdrive, leaving him highly sensitive to smells, loud sounds, or a sudden touch. From his first week of life, he was colicky and inconsolable. In his toddler years, he was tormented by simple tasks like pulling on mittens, his socks had to be exactly even or they drove him crazy, and a scratchy label on the neck of his SpongeBob T-shirt could ignite a colossal, two-hour meltdown. Now, at age five, he still lives in the grip of stormy emotions.

Sarah sighs, scrapes the skillet clean, turns down the burner and starts over with a fresh pat of butter. Zach wants his pancakes shaped like a triceratops and Sarah finds, standing in front of the stove facing a hot skillet, that she has absolutely no idea what a triceratops looks like. Are they the ones with the spiny backs?

"MAMA, why can't you remember?" Zach complains in a yell, only he pronounces it *re-nember*. "We just saw the Land Before Time, right? SPIKE is the triceratops." He enunciates the way she imagines an impatient parent might speak to a severely retarded child. She can hear the tears building up in the back of his throat, a thick wall of misery congealing behind his words. *For God's sake.*

"Here," she says, drizzling syrup on the amoeba-like pancakes and setting the plate in front of her son with the utmost gentleness, even though she wants to holler. "Eat your breakfast—we need to get ready to go see Dr. Moe." After throwing his fork on the floor gets absolutely no reaction, Zach eats his pancakes, protesting mightily. Thankfully, there are no tears and no more screaming. Sarah sends him to the bathroom to brush his teeth while she races down the hall to the bedroom to pull on a blouse, pants and sweater, and to hunt for a pair of socks that match. She usually likes to dab a touch of color on her lips; today, however, grape Chapstick will have to do. Back down the hall to check on Zach. He is swaying in front of the sink, singing to himself and playing with the dog's thick golden fur with one hand, head tipped back joyfully, in his own universe.

"Zachary, what are you doing?" Startled out of his reverie, her son shakes his head sheepishly. "Um, I don't know." He can't remember why he is standing in the bathroom, or what he is supposed to be doing.

"Brush your teeth, honey," Sarah shoos the dog away, swabs blue Rugrats toothpaste onto Zach's toothbrush and hands it to her son. "Let's go already! Now!"

Another morning like this one, sometime when Zach was about three, he discovered the sugar bowl on the kitchen table. By the time Sarah and Rowland were out of bed, Zach had lightly dusted everything in the room with sugar: countertops, wine rack, cookbooks on the shelf, the tops of the coffee tins. From a distance, the room looked like a cake decorated by a crazed pastry chef. Then you drew closer and could see the tiny granules clinging to every surface, taking hold. That is exactly how chaos descends, Sarah thinks, day after day—in a fine sprinkle, piling up and up, until there are mountains to climb, everywhere you look, before you can move forward.

She finds the car keys, stuffs Kleenex and Baby wipes and the checkbook and her insurance card into her overflowing purse and pushes Zach's arms into the sleeves of his fleece jacket, and then Zach is crying in the back seat of the car for some reason she has lost track of, and they are on Route 4—*When did I merge onto the highway?*—in a steady stream of traffic rushing south.

She has tried to explain it to her husband, the dissipation that begins the moment she leaves home and continues relentlessly throughout the day, until she falls asleep each night. She runs all day long: to school, to her classes, to the dry cleaners, to pick up Zach at Montessori, to the Safeway to buy broccoli and laundry detergent. It's like trying to sweep up something that keeps on spilling, she said to Row this morning as he grabbed coffee and headed out the door. I spend all day just trying to gather everyone back in.

Stan

Becoming aware of how you swallow is like thinking about breathing. Suddenly you can't do it naturally any more. Your tongue and epiglottis, which have performed in concert without human intervention for sixty-four years, rebel one day and simply refuse to heed the instructions they are receiving from your brain.

Stan listens warily to the gastroenterologist explaining the mechanics of swallowing, the inflammation of tissue, the how and why of his normal functioning interrupted. Every time he swallows it seems to take an absurdly long time for his mouth to empty of saliva. He is aware of the doctor watching him, and all the watching and explaining makes him jittery. Spit gathers in the corners of his mouth and he realizes with embarrassment that he is drooling, grabs his handkerchief and pretends to cough so that he can dab at his mouth.

All he can think is: Cut to the chase, man. What will it take to fight this thing? To get me back to normal? He tastes blood, bitter and metallic, and realizes he has been biting the inside of his cheek. The doctor is reciting survival statistics now; the numbers are not good. He would really appreciate it if this young man—who looks about thirty, young enough to marry one of Stan's daughters—would simply state the facts. Stan is excellent with facts. He is a lawyer, used to dissecting evidence with a sharp eye for inconsistency or half-truth. If all the facts were laid bare before him in an organized fashion, he feels certain he could find his way out. He wishes the doctor would hurry, would skip the usual speech about "getting your affairs in order" and "talking to loved ones."

He leaves the doctor's office, fighting back an overwhelming urge for a Lucky Strike.

Sarah

The Hyundai Sonata is a sturdy little car, Rowland is always telling people it is, proudly—*I bought my wife a sturdy little car*—and Sarah is convinced he's right, but just now the Sonata feels more like the Tilt-a-Whirl ride at Rockaway Park, with its sticky red leather seats that spun in long delicious circles and left her light-headed and slightly off balance for the rest of the day. Today she feels a bit like someone has dropped her, unceremoniously and without explaining much at all, into the middle of morning rush hour somewhere in southern Maryland. She vaguely remembers that Zach has a doctor's appointment and that they are running late.

A trip to the pediatrician should be a pleasure, really, she reminds herself. A chance to record progress, one of those rare occasions when you can measure change in motion: a child growing up, bone and muscle and skin answering to an invisible plan. Sarah, however, hates doctors. Their offices are swamped with germs, and they are programmed to find things wrong with you.

Traffic is stalled for a half mile before her turnoff. She stares at the bumper stickers on the cars ahead of her: *Work hard, pray hard. Focus on Jesus. In case of Rapture, this vehicle will be unmanned.* Sarah has always scoffed at people who believe in solutions that are small enough to fit onto a bumper sticker. Lately, though, she envies anyone who claims to have faith, people who believe that at any moment the ordinary can become extraordinary, that we might be plucked out of our everyday existence and find ourselves rewarded, after all.

Sarah is stopped at the traffic light, waiting for the left turn arrow to blink green, and closes her eyes for just a moment, her head sinking back against the seat, the day's obligations a roiling sea in her mind. *Dry cleaners, post office, assignment for Ms. Fresno's class, wash Zach's favorite yellow sweatpants, eat more grapefruit, think about taking calcium, pick up milk, English muffins, Tylenol, birthday card for Helene.* When she opens her eyes she finds her car alone in the lane, the light changed already—*how long ago?*—her foot slipped off the clutch pedal. An oversized Toyota pickup passes her on the right, the driver leaning on his horn. Sarah's eyes flee to the rear view mirror, to Zach staring out the window mouthing the lyrics to his favorite song from "Shrek"—he hasn't noticed anything. She is still a good mother.

Stan

Talking to his daughters can be postponed, but Lynda is another story. Stan can tell as soon as he walks into the apartment that his wife is going to get hysterical. She lost a sister to breast cancer two years ago, and the look in her eyes when he begins his explanation is the look of something feral, trapped.

They end up on the sofa holding each other, Stan reassuring Lynda gently that he is not planning to leave her any time soon. His hand shakes slightly when he reaches to pull the crocheted blanket up over his wife's legs, the only sign of the fury that has rocked him since he left the doctor's office. He cannot drink his customary Bloody Mary to numb the anger, because nothing is following custom anymore and tomato juice suddenly gives him wicked heartburn. Over Lynda's teary protests, he mixes himself a strong gin and tonic, adds a slice of fresh lime. Gin is still on the no-no list but not as bad, he reasons, as the tomato juice.

Tanqueray scours his throat going down and he savors the feeling, insists on thinking of it not as damage but as an emblem of victory, the way an athlete might relish the burn in his muscles after a hard-won race. This is what the radiation will feel like. Like a really bad sunburn on the inside of your throat, one of the nurses in the oncologist's office had explained. He takes another long drink and endures the punishing scorch, imagines the gin searing away errant cells.

This is the first lap of my marathon, he thinks, raising his glass silently to Lynda, who is still curled up on the sofa. Feeling the burn, baby. Just starting to feel the burn.

Sarah

The pediatrician's office is crowded and hot when they arrive. The receptionist, whose plastic name tag asks cheerily, "Have you smiled today?" informs Sarah that the doctor is running late, and there are four other patients ahead of them. *Deep yoga breath.* Sarah and Zach tour the waiting room, visit awhile with the tropical fish, play with brightly-colored Legos that are kept in a plastic bin near the "sick child" area. Each time Zach reaches his hand into the bin to pick out a new Lego, Sarah fights back the urge—almost irresistible—to grab it away from him and spray it with Lysol.

"Bowser?" The nurse bungles her name, as always. Sarah gets up with an automatic smile and prepares to walk the twenty feet from her chair to the doorway where Nurse Marie stands waiting smartly. This involves pulling Zach away from his Legos with one hand while she fits the canvas tote bag over her shoulder with the other, and hoists the insurance card and paperwork, two heavy fleece jackets, and her purse, under one arm. Nurse Marie, who holds nothing in her ample arms but a clipboard, watches humorlessly and without offering to help as Sarah makes her way past the receptionist's desk, the bulky canvas bag bouncing crazily against her thigh and Zach yanking with surprising strength on her arm, her purse nudging off her shoulder and threatening at any moment to crash to the floor. "That's okay, I can manage," Sarah mutters under her breath as she approaches the doorway.

"Pardon?" the nurse looks blank and unconcerned. Zach turns to give the Legos one last mournful glance and starts to whimper loudly, digging his heels into the carpet. Sarah wants desperately to smack them both.

The visit is uneventful. Zach weighs 52 pounds, within the normal range for a five-year-old. Sarah remembers another nurse holding him like a plucked chicken when he was a newborn, skinny and naked, and lowering him onto the cold metal infant scale. He has grown to 48 inches, "off the charts," she will report proudly to Row. Nurse Marie raises her eyebrows when Sarah explains that Zach doesn't drink fluoridated water, only spring water, and looks even more disapproving when Sarah says No, she would not like to consider fluoride supplements. Dr. Moe arrives at that point, and takes up the issue of the vaccine for chicken pox. explaining in his kind, patient voice why it is recommended for young children. He sounds, Sarah thinks, an awful lot like Zach this morning with the triceratops.

She will laugh about this with Ginna that evening, she knows. Her best friend in the neighborhood comes over on Fridays after work, to drink wine and talk, and to escape her husband Pat. They'll remark on the insensitivity of doctors, the callousness of Nurse Marie, the power of the medical establishment, the way doctors' offices strip you of all your authority as a mother.

But when Sarah pulls into her driveway that afternoon after work, Ginna's ancient green Volvo is not there. She sees a soft movement in the window—Row parting the curtain to watch for her? —and knows, in that moment, that she is witnessing change in motion, feels the last strong thing within her unravel and fall to the ground.

"Sweet pea." Rowland takes her in his arms, moves her into the living room, lifts the coat from her shoulders. "Your dad called. He had his doctor's appointment today, and they think there may be a mass in his throat. They want to do a biopsy."

"But it was just a sore throat." Sarah's hand finds the edge of the sofa. For more than a month her father has complained of a persistent sore throat, his voice hoarse on the phone, a cough that wouldn't go away. Three weeks ago they sat around a big table at The Palm in New York City, eating steak and creamed spinach, and she had noticed her father's wince when he swallowed, the way he tried to cover it with a cough into his white linen napkin. He was a reformed smoker—two packs of Lucky Strikes a day since he turned sixteen—so coughing wasn't anything unusual, was it?

"Well." In times of crisis Rowland tends to hug Sarah's shoulders too tightly. "Let's just hope everything will be OK." Sarah hates her husband in that instant with a concentrated, glittering ferocity for his downcast face and the sympathy in his eyes. She is too tired to be alarmed by this new feeling; instead, she tucks it away, measuring for a moment its cold weight against the inside walls of her chest.

After she calls her father on the phone and hears the fear sliding behind their conversation, Sarah can do nothing but lie awake and watch the darkness fall outside her bedroom window. She expects, when she closes her eyes, to hear the roar of the house crumbling down around her, evidence of brick and mortar and timbers knocked suddenly loose.

She hears instead the shout of her heartbeat, Row's even, familiar breathing beside her, and on the floor a thud and an enormous sigh as Connie, their dog, settles himself noisily on his blanket for another night.

Stan

A man wakes up to discover he has no voice. It's like being inside a damn Kafka novel, Stan growls to himself as he stretches his legs and tries, painfully, to turn his head and look around the hospital room. He wishes he could growl out loud, wants desperately to yell, to snarl, to bellow, to utter any one of the animal noises that are rising in his throat.

He tries to cough, to see if he can produce even a small sound, and the sudden jolt of pain stuns him, sends him back against the pillow, hard. They have told him not to try to speak for at least a week, to let his larynx heal. The enforced silence terrifies Stan. Inside his head it is anything but silent—his words pour on steadily like breaths, each one inflicting fresh pressure against his skull, a mounting tide of words clamoring for release.

Lynda always describes him as "a word person." In the jubilant haze of post-op medication, Stan realizes he only now truly understands what this means. Stan is a word person in the deepest sense. It's not just that he loves the crossword puzzle in the Sunday Times and can decipher the Daily Cryptogram in under thirty seconds. Those are skills he is convinced anyone with half a brain can master.

For Stan words are more than a game or a tool, they are his currency, his religion. He depends on his words. He doesn't know where he exists in the world without them.

He looks around, taking stock of where he is in this room. There is a pulse monitor clamped to his finger and one IV line flowing into his arm, attached to a contraption on wheels, so he is mobile. Stan feels a slight urge to pee and wonders fleetingly if he should call a nurse, then rejects that idea. He shifts his legs around to one side of the bed and touches a socked foot to the floor, moving with exquisite care. So far so good. Stan slides to a standing position, gingerly, and shuffles over the tiny bathroom. Shuffles! There's a word he didn't think would apply to him until he was about 95 years old. And only a 16-pointer in Scrabble.

Peeing is evidently out of the question. Nothing in his body seems to want to function normally. Stan's legs are suddenly shaking uncontrollably and he grips the metal sink basin in the bathroom for support and stares around the room, avoiding his own face in the mirror. He notices a pink plastic basin with soap, toothbrush, and a razor, and lifts the razor for a moment, testing the blade with one finger. A clear picture comes to him then of what he must do: bring the razor to his throat and cut out the growth that doesn't belong there. Butcher the damned thing before it butchers him. He has seen anatomical diagrams—if he shaved away his skin and tissue, one layer at a time, couldn't he get down to the truth of it all? He needs to touch it, to feel where this madness all began, to assess for himself the kind of purchase it might have on him.

A wave of nausea and chills steals even these momentary thoughts of victory. Stan tries to call out and is again rocketed by pain, doubled over as he lands, hard, on the toilet seat and rests his forehead on the cool rim of the sink, managing to bang loudly with the knuckles of his left hand—the one without the IV—against the metal basin.

Stan finds himself tucked back into bed some time later, pain medication blissfully flowing through his IV bag. He reaches for the remote control and turns on the television above his bed. Cable television news is so insipid it infuriates him: Jennifer Lopez and Ben Affleck are engaged, another big corporation files for chapter 11 after inflating its profits. He flips foggily through the channels until he finds Giada de Laurentis leaning over a steaming platter of eggplant parmigiana, her lips wide and luscious. For the next hour Stan watches cooking shows, his eyes following spoonsful of sautéed vegetables gleaming with oil, mesmerized by peppercorn-crusted roasts and freshly-baked cinnamon rolls piped with white icing. "Giada," the narrator intones, "enjoys long walks on the beach and yoga. She always keeps a secret stash of green tea and dark chocolate in her purse, just for emergencies." Well, Stan thinks, isn't that remarkable. With the promise of more fun facts about his favorite Food Network star, Stan is finally lulled back into sleep.

Sarah

Every time Sarah remembers the night of the operation—the surgeon coming out, finally, to speak to them after long hours of waiting—the gentle gravity in his eyes is a rock pulling her under. "A very large tumor." "Grown significantly." "Recommending radiation although you should know that it can be extremely dangerous. . . life-threatening..." She stood beside her sister Abby and Lynda, listening numbly as the surgeon explained that he had performed a radical procedure, one that had been attempted at only two hospitals in the nation. He had removed half of their father's tongue and his entire swallowing tube all the way down to his voice box, but had taken only part of the larynx so that there was still some hope that he might speak. Someday. With months and months of physical therapy.

This, above all, was what terrified her father: that he might lose his voice. The moment he awoke from surgery he had reached for the nurse's hand, grabbed her, needing urgently to know. Gesturing to his throat, his lips, chapped and bloody: *Voice box?* he mouthed. *Did he take the voice box?*

He floated in and out of sleep for more than a day, his body needing far longer to recover than the doctors had anticipated. Each time his eyes opened, Sarah could see that the fog of anesthesia had erased the answer to his question. His eyes flitted in panic to the side, then found her face and groped wildly for focus. Each time after she answered, utter relief filled his face, enveloped his entire body. Sarah wanted to watch it again and again, the split second when her father believed that he would speak, his eyes shutting reverently, the shudder of his shoulders, the tear marking the same salty track from his cheek down to the white hospital pillow. It was like seeing Zach's face on Christmas morning last year, when he had just turned five and still believed—only barely—in Santa Claus. The moment when he ran uncertainly down the stairs to discover the mound of brightly-wrapped presents and joy flooded his young, open face, when he knew that the miracle had happened one more time.

They all lived in the giddy embrace of Daddy's miracle for awhile. He sat up eventually, let the nurse show him how to take out the tracheostomy tube and clean it with saline solution and a long brush with tiny wire bristles. They learned the language of feeding tubes, suctioning, survival rates. There would be post-op radiation in six weeks, an "eating trial" in a month to see if he could manage food with his reconstructed mouth and tongue. *Wait and see,* the surgeon and the nurses kept urging in quiet, deliberate voices. *We'll just have to wait and see.* For a week, Sarah's father lay in his hospital bed watching television and scrawling instructions and random thoughts in long, impatient, loopy letters on yellow legal pads that were strewn all over the bed. "Cold," he wrote, "need more blankets." "I really love Lynda," he scribbled another day, when Sarah had been sitting with him for an hour or so. "Didn't realize how much until this happened."

Today, he has slept for most of the day. Sarah is staying with him while Abby and Lynda get lunch. She watches her father's face for signs of pain or discomfort and makes one silent resolution after another: I will lose weight, Daddy, I will love my husband more, I will be the daughter you can be proud of.

Once she is sure he is resting comfortably, she gets up and walks to the tiny bathroom stall in the hallway to splash cool water on her face. *Nearly forty years old,* she thinks, peering at herself in the mirror, *and still trying to make my daddy proud. Grow up, woman.*

Back in her father's hospital room the wall of monitors blinks and beeps, registering heart rhythms, pulse rate, blood pressure, oxygen levels. The numbers slide in and out of Sarah's brain like jelly, slippery and elusive.

When Sarah was little, she had a problem with numbers. It was hard for her to tell time or to remember what day of the month it was. Her mother hung a Winnie the Pooh calendar on her bedroom wall, and every night she handed Sarah a fat blue Magic Marker to cross off another day. Together they counted out the number of days left in the week, her mother's hand guiding Sarah's over the calendar's big squares. It did no good, really. By the next morning in school when she was supposed to fill in the date at the top of her spelling worksheet, Sarah's memory would be a perfect blank.

She knew her parents discussed her problem. She heard their hushed voices at the dinner table late at night, long after she and Abby had been tucked into bed. One night, after a conference with Sarah's second grade teacher, her father exploded. "I don't understand it, Evie," he yelled in a stage whisper to his wife, slamming a hand on the table in frustration, "How can she be so stupid?" Sarah lay perfectly

22

still in her bed, the sheets bunched into a tight, sweaty wad underneath her. So there it was, the bald truth, which really wasn't a surprise: her father believed she was stupid.

She has been here for four days and will stay until the end of the week, the hours melting into each other so that, like her second-grade self, she is not exactly sure what day it is. From his hospital bed, her father watches cooking shows and PBS. One day he sees a documentary about whale-watching in Alaska, and fills a page exclaiming in big black letters, "TRIP TO ALASKA! Cruise. Always wanted to go there!!" and an hour later, "Want to get a puppy when I get home. Golden retriever."

Sarah watches his determination and tries to believe in it. She flies home on Sunday and tells Row and Zach that Grandpa is doing amazingly well, it's a miracle, really, that the doctors think he has a chance to learn to speak again, and he might even eat on his own someday. She goes out to a bookstore and buys travel guides to Alaska, books on how to choose a puppy, wraps them in tissue and sends them in a package to her father's apartment with a cheery note urging him to keep the faith.

Tonight, with everyone else asleep, she sinks into her favorite chair in the living room and stares out the window at nothing. *I would like to go to Alaska*, she thinks, picturing a remote fishing village where the days are ruled by snow and wind. Her thoughts cut loose like dogs from a pen, running in circles. She listens for the rustle of trees moving in the darkness outside, realizes she no longer knows where the dangers lurk out there, or what to do about them. The night would come again and again no matter what, Row and Zach were either safe in their beds or they weren't. What could she really do about it? She tries a deep yoga breath, finds that air has somehow clotted in her throat. Drawing only shallow breaths, she wants to call out for Row but she cannot, words seemed to be jammed in her throat also. She feels their mute pressure against her lips and manages with all her strength not to scream. Connie pads into the room and stands at attention beside her, sensing an unknown menace. For the rest of the night, Sarah sits wrapped silently in a quilt in the darkened living room, rocking slowly against the dog's solid, silky strength, allowing the tears to come, willing the blackness to sink down around her, pretending she has chosen to make it night. Pretending that black is the only color she has ever wanted.

Stan

When Lynda arrives at the hospital the next day Stan has been waiting for her for an hour. He motions for her to set up her laptop, then scrolls impatiently until he comes to the page he is looking for, the Herman Miller furniture website. Here it is: the lounge chair designed in 1956 by Charles and Ray Eames, the most inventive furniture designers of his generation. They had taken plywood and bent it, molded it into the precise, supple curves of this exquisite chair, then sheathed it in leather. Charles Eames said his greatest desire was for their chair to feel like "a well-oiled baseball mitt." The chair embodies comfort and utter luxury wrapped up together. Stan stabs a finger at the screen, shaking his head.

Lynda sips her coffee, looks at him quizzically, waiting a beat. "We're buying chairs?"

Walnut? White ash? He points to the choice of finishes on the screen. Lynda smiles slightly, uncertainly, and then gives in to Stan's enthusiasm. He can smell her green apple shampoo when she leans over him briefly to point to the chair she likes, and the deep sweet scent makes him unaccountably happy. Lynda has chosen exactly the wood he would have picked, the oiled santos palisander, with its rich, deeply textured grain. He and his previous wives could never agree on furniture. When he and Evie got married Stan was still in law school, and they pieced together a household from local thrift shops and a friend's castoff linens and pottery. Even after they moved to the suburbs, Evie had never really taken to decorating the house. Then Wife Number Two came along and tried to bury him with her overly fussy Victorian sofas and acres of plaid upholstery. Neither of them had ever appreciated Stan's love of modern design.

He waves at the screen. There is no arguing with the brilliance of this chair. *Time* magazine declared it the "greatest design of the 20th century," with its sleek, elegant curves and streamlined look. The chair won accolades for modern design—ahead of the Swatch Watch and the S-1 steam locomotive, for God's sake. Stan has heard that the original lounge chairs, designed in Brazilian rosewood veneer, now sell for as much as $7,000 each.

Lynda doesn't seem to understand the meaning of his wave. "BUY IT!" Stan scrawls in big, excited letters on his notepad. When he glances up at his wife's face he sees the precise second when everything falters.

Lynda pushes a strand of hair away from her eyes. "I don't know, Stan," she begins. He can taste the quickening, her faith set against his.

He tries to make light of it, scribbling, "It's only money, honey!" When that doesn't bring a smile to Lynda's face he turns away and stares stonily at the screen.

Stan is not about to let a moment like this pass him by. If he is going to battle this damned thing, he requires beauty to fortify himself. He will need to be surrounded by grandeur, by power, by lines that are true, something that he can hold fast to. He vows to buy the lounge chair for his law office as soon as he gets the hell out of here—the santos palisander in orchid white leather. With a matching ottoman.

Sarah

There is an enclosed space at the far end of Ginna's back yard, out of sight from the house, where Sarah stores her rock collection. Over the years she has accumulated hundreds of rocks, gathering them from creekbeds and beaches along the Chesapeake Bay: smooth, polished pieces of quartz and coral, large river stones and slabs of granite. There are fossils along the cliffs near Ginna's house that date back to the Miocene Era, 17 million years ago, when giant sharks and sea turtles swam in the warm waters above what is now southern Maryland. Their endurance captivates Sarah, the way these shards of history have remained embedded in the landscape around her. Some of the rocks that Sarah collects find a place in her garden or in Ginna's, forming irregular ornamental borders or low, altar-like structures that rise like Japanese tea tables from the bee balm and the black-eyed Susans. When Ginna and Pat had a new patio put in two years ago, Sarah designed it, combining round creek stones and angular pieces of slate to create a space that felt at once wild and contained.

The two friends sit in Adirondack chairs near a low stone table that Sarah built here last summer. It is a rough circle of stones, hauled up from a nearby creek, with two flat, almost oblong grey boulders forming a tabletop that rests in Ginna's yard like an ancestral fire pit or the entrance to a Kyoto temple.

Ginna puts her feet up on one of the flat stones. "Pat is having an affair, I know it."

Sarah sighs. "Sweetie, he's not having an affair." Pat Boyle is the most uninteresting man she knows. He works at the Museum of Natural History, where he is an expert on an obscure kind of Brazilian flying beetle. He can talk with great animation about insects and their seasonal migration patterns, and has nothing much to say on any other subject.

"I found something in his wallet," Ginna insists. "A receipt from the dry cleaners."

This is beginning to sound like a bad TV movie. "So?"

"So, he never takes his own stuff to the cleaners." Ginna is practically yelling. "He always leaves it for me. He must be trying to hide something."

There is one completely irrational thing about Ginna, and this is it: the way she worries that her husband—the most boring man on the planet—is about to leave her.

"Ginna. Pat isn't hiding anything. You know that. Besides, you can always tell where he's been."

It's Ginna's favorite joke about her husband. He leaves evidence wherever he goes, forgetting small things like turning off the water faucet, closing drawers, retrieving his toast from the toaster. Ginna wakes up most mornings to a kitchen with drawers pulled open and cabinet doors left ajar, perhaps a half gallon of orange juice sitting on the counter where Pat poured himself a late night drink. "At least I always know where he's been," she remarks with a smile. "Most wives would be thankful for that."

Nobody but Ginna, Sarah thinks, *would be thankful to be married to Pat.*

Ginna changes the subject. "How's your dad?"

"He's OK, I guess. Well, I mean, he's dying."

"I know, honey, I know."

"We're supposed to survive this, right?" Sarah asks after a pause. "Humans are meant to outlive our parents, I know. I just don't see how we're supposed to get through it. Whoever set things up this way. . ."

"It's a stupid system." Ginna agrees quietly, and Sarah loves her fiercely. When they hug goodbye, she grips her friend's shoulders so hard her arms ache, holding her for an extra moment, like something that might save her.

The plan is for Sarah to bring her father home from the hospital ten days later. Abby has been staying at his apartment and helping Lynda, showing up at the hospital every day for a week. She returns to Seattle today, back to her husband and her job with the Seattle Philharmonic. They talk briefly on the phone as Sarah waits to board an early morning shuttle to La Guardia.

"How is he?" she asks her sister.

Abby breathes noisily into the phone. "They keep saying it's too early to tell, and saying the odds aren't very good, but…"

"What?"

"Well, you know Daddy. He's convinced himself that he's going to beat the odds. He says somebody has to be in the 50% who survive."

"Maybe he's right."

"Yeah." Abby sounds irritated, ready to get off the phone. She is the daughter who moved clear across the country to start her own life after college. She ran out of patience with their father long ago.

"Listen, Sarah, Lynda has been at the hospital for six days straight without a break. She'll be glad when you get there."

"I'll be there soon." Sarah promises after a pause.

"Okay. Bye."

Stan

The charge nurse does not want to let Stan go until he and Sarah meet with the social worker one last time to review post-op procedures. "Now you know how to take your trach out by yourself, the way we showed you, right, Mr. Gershman?" Stan nods and waves her away, not bothering to hide his irritation.

The social worker turns to Sarah next. She is young and pretty, with brown hair pulled back into a fresh ponytail, and looks like she has never been sick a day in her life. "Do you have any questions?" Stan is certain that Sarah has a thousand questions. "No, thank you," his daughter manages to say. Stan is scribbling on his pad in large thick letters: "WHEN CAN I GO HOME?"

Finally, the social worker leaves and the nurse returns with the discharge instructions. Although Stan is right there—and he is the patient, after all—the medical staff all talk to Sarah instead, handing her prescriptions, medications, bottles of saline solution, hydrogen peroxide, and tracheostomy supplies. Stan grabs his notepad and writes, "HEY—they took my tongue, not my ears." But in truth he is relieved to see his daughter taking notes, writing down all of the detailed instructions he is sure to forget.

His first steps onto the sidewalk outside the hospital are wobbly and uncertain. The exertion makes his breath ragged and starts his mouth streaming saliva, which requires stopping to fumble for a napkin and blotting his lips and chin in the freezing cold air. Sarah hails a cab and helps him in, then in an awful moment Stan realizes that she will have to give directions to the driver. Stan, who has commanded every courtroom, every restaurant, every stage in his adult life, sits back heavily, mopping at his chin while his daughter names the address: "Eleven-sixty-five Park Avenue, please." All the way down Fifth Avenue the cab is thick with the sounds of Stan's respiration, harsh and gurgling, so unlike human breathing that the cab driver keeps cutting his eyes to the rear-view mirror, to see what kind of freak is riding in his car. Sarah keeps her hand pressed on top of Stan's for the entire drive.

Stan stares out the window and thinks about his grandson. Whenever Zachary visits, Stan pulls out the big road atlas to look at where New York City is situated and to name the places that Zach has visited, a pastime the little boy never grows tired of. "Grampa," he had announced matter-of-factly on his last visit, noticing the year—2002—on the atlas, "I know why they need to make new maps every year, do you? Because the countries are moving closer together all the time, and by next year China might be smashing into America! Then the map would be all wrong." Stan has the sense that things have already happened the way Zach imagines them: continents colliding, the map of the world now rendered utterly useless.

Leon, the doorman in Stan's building, jumps up to help them into the lobby. His arm rests solicitously against the small of Stan's back. "How are you, sir, how are you? Good to have you back." He is shouting, as if Stan has suddenly gone deaf, and his kind, loud voice echoing in the lobby makes Stan's head ache. Leon motions to Sarah that the pharmacy has already made a delivery. "The boxes are right here, I'll have them brought right up," he says brightly. Stan walks by Leon without a sound and heads for the bank of elevators, where he leans wearily against the wall and waits for his daughter.

It will be awhile before they are comfortable with all of the new equipment, Stan can see at once. Sarah sets up the humidifier that the nurse recommended, places the suctioning machine on Stan's side of the bed and fills the plastic chamber carefully with water, begins clearing space in his nighttable drawers for extra suctioning tubes, wire cleaning brushes, plastic bottles of saline, gauze pads. All Stan can think is: Lynda will hate all this clutter.

Sarah goes into the bathroom to set up supplies, and Stan kicks off his shoes and sits down, grateful for his own bed, the smooth, cool sheets. A cough seizes him then and he reaches for his handkerchief, producing an alarming glob of phlegm. He can't catch his breath suddenly—each inhalation brings more phlegm and fluid into his mouth, as if he is trying to breathe through a wall of Jello

Where the hell is Sarah? His instinct is to call her, but his raw throat produces only a gargle. Stan pounds his fist on the nighttable, over and over again, and Sarah rushes over to him. "Daddy. Are you okay?"

Stan shakes his head, wheezing, a little panicky. His trach tube needs cleaning out. They manage to remember the nurse's instructions, and Sarah tugs the slippery metal—which releases with a harsh sucking sound—out of the hole in Stan's neck and rinses it carefully in two different solutions. Hydrogen peroxide, then saline. Bits of blood and flesh spin away down the drain.

Gone Bolshevik

It exhausts Stan to let his daughter take care of him. All he wants now is for her to get the hell out of his room so he can sleep. Lynda will be here at five-thirty or six, and Sarah needs to leave for the airport by seven, so that she can catch the last Delta shuttle home. His daughter stands awkwardly outside his bedroom door while Stan takes off his pants, then she comes in to say good-bye. Stan has already sunken into the sheets, his face turned away from her.

Sarah

The snow has just started to fall when Sarah leaves her father's building, the reflection from the streetlights on Park Avenue sparkling in the blowing snow. It's the kind of evening that makes you feel glad to be inside and cocooned with the ones you love, but Sarah is relieved just now to be outdoors and alone, to tilt her face up and feel the damp flakes on her cheeks, to be enveloped by the soft, penetrating white of the snowfall and the surrounding din of New York City traffic, the movements of people heading home. After the close air of the hospital room, the sharp, slightly sweet smell of human flesh that they carried with them to her father's apartment, she is grateful for the sting of cold air filling her lungs. Then she is a child suddenly—*look, Daddy, I'm swallowing the snow!*—her head tipped back in awe, gulping white air beneath these same streetlamps, laughing in delight. Her father shifting his weight in the cold, his face breaking into a broad smile meant just for her. He was wearing his long camel cashmere overcoat, on his way to work, and she was clasped in her mother's mittened hand, coming home from the park. *That smile,* her teachers and her friends' mothers would say, shaking their heads at how handsome Sarah's daddy was, and she would nod with secret satisfaction.

Gone Bolshevik

Sarah knows she should hail a cab, but instead she begins to walk, following 92nd Street toward Central Park. The streets are emptying as flower vendors pull their merchandise inside, and people on the way home from work buy milk at the corner store or hurry for the shelter of apartment buildings and gaily-lit restaurants. A homeless man approaches her on her solitary walk to the park. He looks only a few years older than Daddy, and she reaches into her purse without hesitation to hand him a dollar. If Row were here, she knows, he would explain why it was sentimental and counterproductive to give money to street people. Rowland glances the other way when they are walking down the street and Sarah gives money to a homeless person. He smooths his hair with that quick little gesture he uses to hide irritation, and his mouth clicks.

The sun is already low and pale in the February sky, and the stone benches along Central Park are empty except for men and women who look lost. Sarah nearly collides with a middle-aged woman standing quietly on the street corner, with a shopping bag full of possessions and a battered cardboard sign that reads, "Homeless mother. Please help." Sarah wants to bring the woman inside with her, to make her hot soup. Instead she reaches hastily into her purse and wordlessly hands the woman a ten-dollar bill. Ten dollars is my handprint on the world, my handhold for today, she told herself that night, grimly. It seemed, for that one moment, to be enough.

Stan

People keep sending him books—self-help manuals, medical journals, books that explain how his cancer would disappear if he would only meditate and eat more whole grains and broccoli. Stan ignores most of them, leaves them stacked in unruly piles on his bedside table or the living room coffee table or in the hallway. Somewhere in the piles, unopened, are the books that Sarah sent him about puppies and traveling in Alaska.

Lynda, who is an excellent cook, especially hates the cookbooks. "What do they think," she fumes each time a new cookbook arrives, wrapped in ribbon, "I should be planning your last meal already?" But Stan notices that lately she has been flipping through the recipes, turning down a page here and there. The *Treasures of Provence* cookbook has been left open on the kitchen table for the past week.

Eating—once a central pleasure of the day—now presents a major challenge. Stan's daily menu consists of soup, applesauce, scrambled eggs, and vanilla Peptamen, a liquid food supplement that tastes like flavored chalk. Once, he managed sesame noodles from the Thai place around the corner. Anything easy to swallow, Lynda can soften or mash until it's the right consistency for him to try a few spoonfuls. All of that mushy food leaves him craving texture: crunchy celery, the snap of green beans in his teeth, a good soft pretzel coated with salt. Potato chips! He actually dreamt about eating potato chips last night, a whole bag of them, the kettle-cooked kind with their edges burnt brown. When he woke up he could taste salt and peanut oil.

Stan leafed through one of the books this morning, a guide to the Grand Canyon. He and Lynda had visited the Canyon once with the girls, and it's a place that fascinates Stan, the way it reveals its entire history, decade by decade, the inner architecture of the past laid bare in brilliant red and orange ribbons of rock. He hasn't bothered to mention to Lynda that he would love to go back there. Stan knows if he brings it up, his wife will look at him like he's suggesting a trip to the moon.

Lynda comes into the room now where Stan is trying to fake sleep, and puts a hand on his shoulder. "Sweetie, would you like to take a walk?" she asks brightly. Her voice is too perky. She has pushed her fear to the side and discovered a relentless cheerfulness, which gives him headaches. He does not want to take a walk. But he wants to make his wife happy. "OK," he scribbles on his notepad, agreeing without enthusiasm, and submits to her help when she slides his jacket on and wraps a scarf tightly around his neck.

Outside, they walk two long blocks to Central Park and then Stan signals with an impatient flick of his hand that he needs to rest. They sit on a stone bench and Stan watches people pass them by—a young Hispanic couple swinging a toddler between them, an elderly woman strolling with her daughter—raging at them silently for their energy, for how quickly they can walk without their legs cramping up, without becoming exhausted. He is insanely jealous of total strangers, of anyone who is healthy. He has become so used to the silent fury humming inside of him that it is as familiar as his constant heartburn, or his wheezy breathing, or the way his neck aches when he turns it, or any of the countless other physical sensations that fill every day.

He will not talk about any of this with his wife or his law partner. Stan refuses to become one of the over-sixty crowd, the *alte kakers* who spend their time comparing medical symptoms and recounting trips to their numerous doctors' offices. He has in fact guarded against just that since he turned sixty, when he became aware that everyone around him—at the office, on the subway, at dinner parties, for God's sake, was joining in this chorus of decline without realizing how ridiculous and dreary they all sounded. As if life from now on was supposed to be nothing but a long, slow and steady slide downhill.

After a moment he becomes aware that his wife is looking at him, and he shrugs his shoulders upward in exaggerated irritation. "What?" his eyes demand.

"Look. It's a beautiful day." Lynda says with a sigh. "I just thought maybe you could try to feel a little, I don't know... happy."

Stan's mouth tightens. He fishes around in his jacket pocket for his notebook, finds a felt tip pen. "Nice day," he writes in small, clipped black letters. "I love every petal on every flower. OK?" He tosses the pen down on the bench, thrusts the notepad toward his wife.

Lynda stares at the words for a second. "Jesus," she says, and gets up to walk back towards the apartment. Stan watches her go until her blue wool coat is lost in the swirl of people moving around him on the street and a tiny spark of panic flares inside him at the realization that he has been left here alone, on a bench. But immediately after the panic recedes, another feeling rushes in: peace. This may be the first time he has been alone since he came home from the hospital. Nobody watching every breath he takes. Nobody telling him when to eat and drink and piss. Nobody insisting on talking about cancer.

He doesn't really believe in the cancer, that's his problem. It's not something you can see or touch, like poison ivy or the chicken pox. When the girls got chicken pox, he remembers watching the vigorous spread of scabby red bumps across their arms and chests, the scars that marked their skin for months afterward, clear evidence of the disease. Evidence: that's what he believes in. He doesn't know how to confront an opponent he can't even see. This thing he has, it doesn't feel much worse than a bad sore throat or the flu, and he's supposed to respect it, to believe it has the strength to finish him?

He has put doctors up on the stand, many of them, and he knows how easily medical truth can be distorted. He thinks about the miners he met in West Virginia, their lungs clogged with tar from years of inhaling coal dust down underground. Most of those men could barely breathe, and the coal companies hired doctors to take the stand as expert witnesses. Day after day they sat there in the courtroom, denying that years spent in the mines had anything at all to do with the workers' symptoms. Citing medical evidence. That was back in the 1960s, when nobody knew about Black Lung Disease, and Stan had been a kind of pioneer, taking on the coal companies and fighting for worker's compensation laws. He shakes his head, thinks he hasn't felt like a pioneer in a long time.

When he looked in the bathroom mirror this morning he saw only this: a middle-aged man wincing while brushing his yellow teeth, the smell of rot rising from his throat. A man whose courtroom speeches were once legendary, now only able to make growling noises and to cough up spectacular amounts of phlegm.

One of the books piled up in the apartment is from Dick, his old law partner. It explains cancer as the body out of harmony with life's creative processes. A group of cells in the body gone haywire, in retribution for something done wrong in a past life. Cancer as bad karma. Dick's wife Vivian must have picked that one out—she's a real flake. Stan doesn't think like that, doesn't believe in illness as payback. Doesn't believe in a just universe at all, really.

The smell of roasted peanuts makes him look up and— painfully, deliberately—turn his head. A rough, gritty smell that finds his nostrils and lays there, slowly filling his mouth and punching the back of his throat with longing. The man selling peanuts is scooping them, hot and still in their shells, into white paper bags, his arm working at lightning speed, a line of customers already forming in front of his cart. Stan watches them with unspeakable envy. If he acknowledges the cancer at all, it is here, now, in this diminishment of his desires. One day you're dreaming of visiting the Great Wall of China, or testifying before the Supreme Court...the next day, life would feel complete if you could only chew and swallow some fresh roasted peanuts.

"Stan."

He looks up and sees that Lynda has come back for him.

There are advantages to not being able to speak, he decides. He is grateful that he doesn't have to say anything, doesn't need to explain the hot return of his fury. Or the relief that floods him at the same time, unclenching hands that he had balled up in his lap without even knowing it. A gust of cold wind blows across the street and Stan ducks his face down inside his scarf, glad for an excuse to turn away from his wife. He sends one last furtive glance in the direction of the peanut cart before he heaves himself up from the bench and silently, slowly, begins the walk back home.

Sarah

B y the time you lose your parents, you are supposed to be grown
up enough to handle it, Sarah knows. The only thing nobody
tells you is that your entire body will hurt when you wake up every
morning, worse than when you have the flu. And that your father, who
is about to die, will visit your dreams at night, mumbling incoherently
like a madman or a drunk on the street.

Last night, she stuck earplugs in both ears and pressed her eyes
tightly closed beneath her sleep mask, hoping she could shut out the
dreams, but there they were anyway: Daddy riding bareback on a black
horse along steep cliffs; camping alone in a giant, dense Amazonian
rain forest; maneuvering his bicycle through New York City traffic with
daredevil flair. The dreams always end the same way, with her father
staring directly into Sarah's eyes and shaking a finger at her while he
tries to tell her something. "Trick yaks," he seemed to be saying
urgently in last night's dream. "Murky softballs. Sopty, molty pretzels."

Sarah has no idea what the dreams mean. She opens a bag of
pretzels, eats them for breakfast. Maybe if she does what he says, he
will go away. Maybe if she keeps dreaming him, he won't ever go away.

Her ache to hear her father's voice is more powerful than she
could have imagined. It is deeper—Sarah is ashamed to say it—far

deeper than sex, more like her yearning for her son when he was an infant. She can remember the physical imprint that Zach as a baby left on her skin, the way his damp head fit into the space between her neck and her shoulder, leaving her with a hollow, scooped-out sense of loss when he was lifted from her into someone else's arms. This is the same keen ache, gnawing at her sleep, filling her with a restless desperation, the kind of physical longing she imagines could make someone jump off a very high bridge to slice into icy dark waters below. When, at the end of her father's first week home, she calls the apartment and has to speak to him through Dani, an Ethiopian nurse who doesn't know her father and has never even heard his true voice, Sarah abruptly hangs up the phone. Rowland has to talk her out of jumping immediately on a train to New York. Sarah knows that she has utterly lost her bearings. The single thing she has relied on to be her compass—the sound of home—can no longer take her there.

　　Her father has resumed going to work at his law practice now, at least one or two half days each week. On Monday mornings, when she knows that he and Lynda will both be at the office, Sarah dials the apartment phone number just to hear his voice on the old answering machine message. It is scratchy and rough and dearly familiar—and gone as irrevocably as the voice of someone who has died. The guttural, jerky mumblings her father can manage now, after enduring a few weeks of speech therapy, will never smooth themselves out into quite those particular sounds she is listening to now, punching in the number again and again.

　　She hears him speaking at odd moments, like the twinge of a phantom limb. His voice echoes in her mind, the way for months after her first dog Ruby was struck by a car, she could hear over and over again the exact high yip the dog made going under the wheels. Her father had been visiting her at college that day. He stood in her apartment in his white boxers smoking the morning's first cigarette, when she stumbled through the door holding Ruby, wrapped in her jacket. "You better get that dog to a vet," Daddy advised. "She doesn't look so good." Sarah drove the ten careening miles to the veterinary hospital with one hand on the steering wheel and the other bracing the dog, whose head was lolling crazily in the front seat, her breath catching in funny little gasps. It wasn't the gasping sound that stayed with Sarah afterward, though, but that last piercing yelp in the split second before the car hit, before Ruby felt the impact. It was the sound of something before it happened, before the future shouted its name.

Stan

On November 20, 1968, a huge explosion ripped through Consolidated Coal's Mine Number 9 near Farmington, West Virginia. The explosion was so powerful that people eating in a diner twelve miles away reported feeling the tremors from the blast. Ninety-nine coal miners were trapped underground, and only 21 ever made it to the surface alive. The bodies of many of the other 78 remained entombed deep inside the earth and were never recovered. The Farmington disaster, as it came to be called in the national press, was judged to be the result of a massive methane eruption.

Stan was working for the U.S. Senate when the explosion happened, serving as Minority Counsel to the Senate Committee on Labor and Public Welfare. His job was to advise the Committee on labor issues, which involved mastering the research available on any subject related to workers' health, safety, or compensation. In 1966, when Stan moved his family to Washington, D.C. to take the Senate job, the hot issues were unions and mine safety.

Stan traveled to West Virginia and went down in the mines, toured the underground tunnels and the narrow black shafts where miners spent their days. When he returned to the office, he wrote the first draft of what would become the Coal Mine Safety Act of 1969. The language of the Act was bold; it deplored the "disgraceful health and safety record" of the coal mining business, and put in place strict safety regulations and protections for victims of Black Lung.

To Stan, the coal miners he met were nearly mythic figures. Here were men who spent hours in an underground world doing backbreaking, relentless work, emerging blackened, dusty and spent at the end of a ten or twelve-hour shift. And yet they were part of a bold and triumphant process, an industry that extracted energy from sheer rock. Coal was hauled up from the bowels of the earth and transformed into fuel that powered an entire nation. Whenever Stan watched a freight train clatter by, carrying coal from small mountain towns to the shipyard in Newport News, he knew he was a witness to something momentous. He felt what a marvelous feat it was, man's conquest of ferocious nature, over the forces that tried—but failed—to overtake us. To an idealistic young attorney, miners were the symbols of both the might and the brutality of American industry. He shook his head at the faith that must keep men like that going.

In every job, if you're lucky, there is a home run, an accomplishment that becomes the standard against which everything else afterwards will be judged. The Mine Safety Act was a home run with the bases loaded. Sitting in his office now, Stan is at a loss to think of anything he has achieved since then that even comes close. He has measured himself against those coal miners, if truth be told. He has wondered what he would ever accomplish that could match their heroic strength or could bring the same gritty satisfaction he imagined they gained from their labor, lying down beside their wives at night with aching shoulders and skin crusted grey from coal dust.

Now he feels a stab of pain in his neck and flinches at his own weakness. For this task—beating cancer—he doesn't know what he's supposed to measure. How well he endures pain? How stoic his smile when people ask how he is feeling? If this is his heroic moment, he is not at all sure that he is up to it.

Stan picks up a jagged black rock that anchors a pile of papers on his desk. It's a piece of coal from Martinsburg, West Virginia, and he holds it in his palm now and closes his fingers tightly around it, as if he could draw out some of the strength compressed in the cold, shiny rock. After one of his West Virginia trips, he had given Sarah and Abby small animal figurines fashioned from chunks of coal, a Scottie dog for Sarah and a horse for Abby. He wonders if the girls still have them. Something to remind them of what their old man did for a living, he thinks morosely. He tosses the chunk of coal into the trash can on his way out of the office.

Sarah

It has only been a little over a month and a half since her father came home from the hospital. Sarah has gone back to work after taking a brief leave of absence. Each morning, after dropping Zach at kindergarten at the local Montessori school, she drives the five miles to Bayview Elementary, says good morning to Rose, the receptionist, walks to her classroom and lines up paints and smocks and easels for the day's teaching units as if she knows what she's doing, as if she belongs anywhere in this new order of things.

Ginna bakes pies for her, a different kind each week. She runs a catering business from her home, and pies are her specialty. Her pies have thick, buttery crusts and the lightest fillings: coconut custard, banana crème, chocolate mousse. Today she has brought over a sweet potato pie warm from the oven.

The two women have known each other for five years, since Sarah and Row bought this house by the Chesapeake Bay. Sarah arrived on Ginna's doorstep one morning with baby Zach bundled in his stroller, to ask if her neighbor wanted to take a walk. Ginna had helped Sarah to stay sane for those first crazed months of endless breastfeeding and sleepless nights and days alone with an infant; had somehow known, although she and her husband did not have children themselves, how much a new mother needs a friend.

Now she stands in Sarah's kitchen preparing to whip cream, taking the beaters and a big mixing bowl out of the freezer and pouring out the thick, heavy cream. The plan is to bring the pie over to Sarah's great aunt Henrietta. Nearly ninety-five, Hen lives in an assisted living facility nearby. Most Saturdays, if Hen is having a good day, Sarah and Zach join her for lunch.

Zach adores Hen with a passion that is inexplicable to Sarah, since the elderly woman cannot play with him or even match his pace when they are walking, she with her heavy metal walker and Zach bouncing along beside her like a puppy, circling back to meet her if he gets too far ahead. He studies her uncritically and delivers his impressions with the uncensored freedom that only children enjoy. "You know, Mom," he observes as they enter the lobby of Hen's building, where several residents are napping in their armchairs, "Old people have necks like iguanas."

Hen is waiting for them in the sun room, a shawl wrapped tightly around her shoulders, even though the day is mild. Sarah leans over to give Hen a kiss on each cheek, and shows her the sweet potato pie. "Ginna baked this just for you."

"Oh, Sarah," her aunt bunches her lips in disgust, "I don't need any more pie. You know I'm supposed to watch my sugar. What did you bring this for?"

Zach looks stricken. Sarah shakes her head and puts the pie plate down on the table near Hen. "You really are turning into a cranky old lady."

They eat in the communal dining room, where the conversation is light. During the week, Sarah tucks away tidbits of information about her son to be shared later: his latest art project at school, a new friend, or new words he has learned. Today, she mentions that she has begun working on a huge rainforest project at the Montessori school. One entire classroom will be turned into a rainforest scene, with papier-mache monkeys swinging from oversized rubber trees, and giant insects crafted from cardboard egg cartons and pipe cleaners.

"Sarah, when do you rest?" Hen's face crinkles, with exasperation or worry, it's hard to tell. "Every time I talk to you, you're busy, busy. The kid is sick, you're taking a yoga class, there's a party to organize, now you're making a rain forest—that's a new one." She takes a careful bite of her roll and waves it in the air for emphasis. "You'd better watch out, kiddo. You'll run yourself ragged."

Sarah adopts the same even tone that she often uses with Zach. "I'm fine, really," she says. "I'm not going to collapse any time soon." She has explained the realities of two-career parenting to her great-aunt a dozen times. All Hen knows is that when she was working at the office of the Amalgamated Meat Cutters' Union, only single girls took jobs outside the home. She cannot fathom how things could have changed so swiftly in the short space of two generations.

Sarah brings out Ginna's pie for dessert, topped with generous dollops of whipped cream. "Well, maybe just a little," Hen sighs grudgingly. "You have to have some pleasures in life." She eats the pie lustily, she and Zach both licking the last drops from their spoons.

Sarah and Ginna finish the pie that afternoon while Zach naps. Sarah digs into the sweet potato filling, treasuring the pungent, spicy taste on her tongue, wondering fleetingly if it was possible to make Peptamen in this wonderful flavor. Her father said he could actually taste the bland vanilla of the liquid supplement he poured into his stomach tube. If Lynda mixed in Pepsi or chicken soup, he claimed there was an aftertaste that reached up into his mouth and nostrils, and was sometimes pleasant.

"You're doing it again, right?" Ginna lays a hand on Sarah's shoulder, part empathy and part admonition.

"Oh, Gin, he can't eat *anything*. He loves food, you know, and all he can taste is that liquid crap." Sarah doesn't bare this truth to anyone else—how often in every day, every hour, she is thinking of her father. She tastes food for him, the way a mother bird does for her baby, chewing it until it is almost liquid, running her tongue over the substance in her mouth and imagining her father drinking it.

All of Sarah's appetites have shut down, one by one. She has no desire to eat or to drink. She sips from a mug of tea or coffee all day long, and only eats when she absolutely has to. The other day at school she was so dizzy with hunger by lunchtime, she almost fainted in the teacher's lounge. She let Rose bring her a package of cheese and peanut butter crackers, and dutifully ate two of them.

Sex with Rowland has become completely mechanical. She lies beneath her husband and mentally makes shopping lists for the pies that she and Ginna will bake the next morning. Or she counts her art supplies, visualizing rows of paintbrushes and small smeared bottles of tempera paints lined up on her students' easels. Last night, thankfully, Row finished on top of her after only three rows of easels.

Rowland thinks she has become obsessed. Sarah heard him the other day, talking in an urgent whisper about her to Ginna. "This can't be healthy." "At least she's eating—my God, in the beginning, I thought she was going to go on a hunger strike until her father could eat again."

Row continues to be baffled by Sarah's pain about her father, by its extraordinary depth and texture. He knows grief, to be sure—he lost his own father to a sudden stroke eight years ago. But his experience of that pain was quick, searing, a skillet-hot flash, and then just as completely, it was over. He mourns in the same way that he conducts everything else in his life, with precision. Row cannot fathom cleaving to grief the way he believes his wife has, coddling it, carrying it—or rather, allowing it to carry her from day to day.

Sarah does not feel as crazy as she sounds when her husband describes her. She resolves that this week, at least, she will stop reading the cancer web sites each day, will cut herself loose from the statistics and survival rates, the daily emails to Abby, the guessing and measuring of how far they have come and how far there is yet to go.

Ginna has never said a word to Sarah about the printouts from cancer journals that blanket her desk, about her odd eating habits since the surgery, or the Monday morning calls to her father's apartment that only she and Sarah know about. Now she moves her chair behind Sarah's and rubs her friend's shoulders. "You, my dear, need a safe place to hide," Ginna says. "A place where you don't let the darkness creep in, even if it's only for an hour."

Whenever Sarah wants to calm Zach, she tells him to picture his favorite place, someplace where he feels peaceful and happy. "Florida!" he always whispers in pleasure, remembering sunlight, the wonder of pelicans, unhurried mornings, his prowess at swimming halfway across the pool underwater when he was only four and a half. If her son is having a particularly bad night, Sarah snuggles up so that her body lies completely alongside his, a faithful shoreline he can lean into, and together they imagine an entire Florida vacation from the beginning: the ride on the airplane, mornings at the beach, his favorite Italian restaurant with the waterfall where he is allowed to order a Sprite, feeding baby monkeys at the Monkey Jungle. By the time they arrive at the baby monkeys, Zach's eyelids are dropping lower and lower, his body melting into hers, believing with a child's perfect faith that you had only to ask and you would always be granted a safe harbor.

The phone rings, startling Sarah out of her reverie. "Yes?"

"Sarah." It's Kathy Rumley, the director of Zach's school. "Zach's fine, don't worry, I just thought you should know he's been behaving a little strangely. He wouldn't come down from the slide when the kids were out on the playground yesterday. Monica doesn't think Zach even heard her calling him, telling him it was time to come down. It's like he was under some kind of spell."

Sarah can picture her son in his green stegosaurus T-shirt, perched high on top of the slide. His hands are holding fast to the cool metal but his face tips upward to take in the whole sky above. Sarah sees the enormous sky opening up for Zach, layers of blue yielding to deeper layers, the scattered clouds rimmed by sunlight. She hears the honk of a stray goose headed for the Bay and knows that Zach is hearing it, too—knows her son is noticing the piercing blue light and the calls of wild things to each other; but he is not hearing the teachers' voice below, insistent and worried: "Zach! Zachary? It's time to come down, now."

"You need to touch him on the shoulder." Sarah says into the phone.

"What?"

"Tell Monica to climb up there next time and touch Zach gently on the shoulder," Sarah explains. "He won't hear you talking to him, he needs physical contact. It brings him back to earth."

There is a long pause at the other end of the line. Finally Kathy says, "I think it would be a good idea for you to come in and see Mrs. Merkin."

"Okay. Fine. I'll see her at lunchtime on Monday." Sarah hangs up impatiently, to find Ginna staring at her again. "What?"

"You must be part Betazoid."

"I have no idea what you're talking about."

"Star Trek. The Betazoids are a species from the planet Betazed, and they are empaths. They sense the emotions of the people who are close to them. Like you and Zach. How did you know touching his shoulder would help?"

Sarah shakes her head. "I'm his mother, it's part of the job description."

She has been explaining Zach to other people for so long she hardly gives it any thought—his temper tantrums, his sensitivity to smell, the way he needs to sort his crayons by color while the other children around him are happily scribbling pictures. The way he sometimes seems to lose track of where he is in space and time.

She wonders, though, if Ginna is right. Sarah cannot help taking into herself the feelings of others. She thinks of it as a special sensitivity or heightened awareness, which she has had as long as she can remember.

When she was eight, she got on an elevator in Hen's building and an older man stepped into the elevator behind them, looking lost. "Hello," Sarah's aunt said with a slight smile. "How are you?" Sarah added, proud that she remembered how to be polite. The man looked directly into her eyes. "My wife died last year." he answered. "So I'm a little lonely all the time." The look on his face cut Sarah to the bone. She felt something inside her collapse a little, close to her rib cage, until it was hard to breathe. Tears pooled in her eyes, and the man gave her a sad smile and a little wave as the elevator stopped on his floor and he shuffled out into the hall.

"Why are you crying?" Hen asked, one hand on Sarah's shoulder, turning to look closely at her. When Sarah explained, her aunt looked at her strangely and didn't say anything more. It was the first time Sarah realized that not everybody experienced other people's feelings as keenly as she did. Not everyone, she reminds herself now, pushing away the sweet potato pie, can eat only pie when their father gets cancer.

Stan

He wants only to hold his grandson's hand. But there is always something clutched in it: pebbles, a dirty piece of moss or tree bark, the plastic top from a magic marker. Stan is not good at this, never has been. When Abby and Sarah were young he often felt he didn't know what to say to his own daughters, and he finds Zachary equally bewildering. So much feeling and energy compressed in those warm little bodies, they make him afraid, as if at any moment—like a science experiment gone awry—they might bubble over.

He could be happy just standing close to Zach now in the toy store. Watching his grandson grab plastic dinosaurs out of the oversized bins and line them up on the floor is pure delight. Zach is carefully placing the creatures together by type, sorting the T-Rexes from the stegosauruses and the triceratops and the ones with the spiny backs that fly. The small boy is utterly absorbed in his task, and this makes his grandfather content. They will be fine, he sees, just like this. It is a relief, really, not to be expected to carry on intelligent conversation with a five-year-old.

Sarah is the one who worries about it the most, that the operation and the tracheostomy tube would frighten Zach, or would distance him from his grandfather. He couldn't talk, it was true, but

they could communicate in other ways. Zach's dinosaurs are marching in a long parade now, headed away from the bins down the store aisle. A sales clerk walks by and smiles, and Stan smiles, too, looking on proudly at the little boy's industry. Sarah should learn not to worry so much.

She had not been so anxious as a little girl. He thinks he can remember many days of laughter, Sarah running to hug him when he arrived home from work. Life was easier then, less freighted with expectations. Evenings in the house after dinner, he would read the newspaper from front page to back while his wife gave the girls a bath and read aloud bedtime stories.

He watched Sarah give Zach a bath, once. Zach in the bathtub melts his heart completely. Something about the slick, skinny naked boy body and how completely he dwells inside of it, with no self-consciousness at all, only joy. Water has always made the boy happy. That particular night, it was a pair of new swim goggles delighting him—Zach pulled them over his eyes, called out *One, Two, Three, Action!* and then pinched his nose shut, gulped air and dunked under the water to see how long he could stay down. Stan watched the small body hang almost motionless in the dim water, a shadow against the white tub. He loved Zach's gleaming wet face breaking through the bathwater an instant later, a huge smile of pride lighting his face. "Mama! Did you see how long I was under? How long was that? It was a whole minute, right?" Stan loved it all: the disappearing and the deliverance, the light of pure joy on the child's face as he surfaced and looked to be sure that his mother was watching.

It always comes back to the physical world. Those fragments

of touch and smell that children give us, he thinks, they are what lasts, what will redeem us. He can still smell the lavender bath soap that Sarah uses, can picture the way it foamed around Zach's shoulders in the tub. He will be saved by these moments, if he can believe in them.

When he feels the clot in his throat he panics just a tiny bit. It is like this each time, the overwhelming sensation that his oxygen is about to be cut off. The nurses had warned him this would happen—the trach tube clogging, usually with his own phlegm—and he ought to be used to it by now. But every time it nearly slays him, making him straighten up suddenly and throw his arms out, as though grabbing for air. He can usually clear the clog out himself, using the long cotton-swabbed sticks they had provided at the hospital. He slides a hand into his jacket pocket, fishes around and produces a plastic-wrapped stick. By now he is accustomed to doing this, finding the hole near his collarbone and plunging the stick in, used to the harsh sucking sound and the discomfort of the metal tube shifting under his skin. The stick comes up coated thickly with phlegm and a little blood, and he wraps it in a Kleenex.

A wheezy cough builds in the back of his throat. Sometimes this happens, the stick by itself isn't enough. He still can't breathe much, can't draw more than a shallow pull of air, and it is making him feel light-headed. He needs to get to a sink, where he can remove the entire trach and flush it with hot water. Hydrogen peroxide and saline, they had instructed him sternly in the hospital, but hot water would have to do for now. Right now.

Zachary. He can't leave the boy alone. He looks quickly around, spies a young woman nearby who looks friendly. Can he trust her? She has a toddler pulling on her arm, and her face shows the weary softness of a young mother's face. "Woooozhoo" comes out of Stan's mouth. She is staring at him now. He gestures toward Zach, sees her look of incomprehension and wrestles down his own impatience and mounting panic. Seeing a display of drawing pads in a nearby aisle, he grabs one and scrawls a note in big letters: "WATCH MY GRANDSON?" and then adds below, "BATHROOM." She nods— he is sure he sees her nod—and just then an enormous cough overtakes him, the pressure in his airway stealing what is left of his breath and making him rush, hunched over and choking, toward the restroom at the back of the store.

When he comes out of the men's room only moments later, dabbing at the water stains that run down the front of his shirt, Sarah is standing in the dinosaur aisle, without Zachary. The young woman and her toddler are nowhere to be seen. Stan has never been aware, before, of just how quickly one act could unravel everything.

Sarah sees him and her face folds inward on itself. She is processing the information that her son is not with his grandfather, that he may be lost somewhere in this vast shopping mall. He knows he has failed, and worse, that his daughter will not give him a second chance. She will not be forgiving where Zach is concerned. What flashes through Stan's mind is: Disneyworld. He wants to take Zach to Disneyworld, he has already begun planning the trip, the colorful resort brochures spread out on the dining room table. Some nights, when he is having trouble sleeping, he sits up in bed looking through the brochures, conjuring images of his grandson in the Magic Kingdom, hugging Mickey Mouse in delight.

He stands alone now next to Zach's small army of dinosaurs, still holding their formation on the store's tile floor. He will not be allowed to take his grandson to Disneyworld. Even if Zachary is found quickly—Stan reasons that he couldn't have gone far, surely he is just in the next aisle—Stan understands that everything has changed. He sees things clearly now: he is just another slowly dying, sick old man with dribble stains on his shirt. He has become one of the men he sees on benches at the boardwalk, staring out over the ocean with eyes that have been emptied of light. Breath clots in his throat, catches in small gasps as he tries to breathe evenly, places one finger over the tube in his esophagus so that he can speak. He wants to explain, he must say something to his daughter. But even he does not recognize the animal sounds that emerge from his mouth as Sarah turns away from him and runs out of the store.

Sarah

Rocks and fossils line the windowsills of Sarah's classroom. Some of them were gifts, a few she purchased as souvenirs—turquoise from Arizona, rose quartz from the mountains of New York—and others she gathered on her walks along the Bay. Her students love the semi-precious stones, especially the cat's eye agate shot through with threads of bright orange, and the sharks' teeth. Sarah has her two personal favorites: a stubby piece of branched white coral from Florida that Zach picked up because he said it looked like a galaxy, and a small black dog carved from a lump of West Virginia coal. The dog had been a gift from her father when Sarah was ten.

She has not seen her father since the toy store incident. They found Zach quickly, thank God, standing in the entrance to another store, mesmerized by a man demonstrating a motorized flying helicopter. "I lost Grampa," Zach said simply when Sarah rushed over and threw her arms around her son. He was fine, but Sarah was so shaken she couldn't speak to her father for the entire ride home.

I can't think about this now. She turns away from the windowsill and the little coal dog and back to the art projects spread on the long, low tables in the center of her room. These are her students' final art projects for the year, and she is supposed to be grading them. She hates working late at school, and generally avoids it, walking out promptly when the 3:20 bell rings even if there are paintbrushes soaking in the deep stainless steel sink and glitter on the floor, even if it means there will be extra work to get her classroom straightened up in the morning. But too often at the end of the year, grading catches up with her, and she has to leave Zach in the after-care room for an hour or more while she finishes her work.

She has hardly ever regretted her decision to take a job teaching art. She is good at teaching. And she loves her students, the first graders with their damp fingers and rapt, eager attention and the older boys with attitude, who slouch in their chairs and are determined to hate art class. She especially enjoys the fifth grade girls, the oldest in the school, who start out at the beginning of the school year so hesitant, and then one day discover that they are really good at painting. Or that they can take a block of gray clay and turn it into something that is wild and surprising and alive.

The end of the school year, however, is the hardest time for Sarah, because she is expected to judge her students, to assign final grades. Grades in elementary school seem a bit absurd to her, anyway. Sarah always tries to get her students not to take them too seriously, to focus instead on creating and appreciating art. "Vincent van Gogh," she announces, "did not get good grades in school. Michelangelo did not get A-pluses." She has no idea if this last statement is true or not, but it impresses the kids. Even the second and third graders have heard, vaguely, of Michelangelo.

She thinks now of how easily her father can render judgment, with a lawyer's vehemence. When Sarah and Abby were in school, he had no difficulty identifying their successes and their failures. Abby was good at the two subjects their father admired the most, mathematics and science, where the rules were clear and precision was possible. Sarah was a complete failure when it came to algebra, trigonometry, or driving the family station wagon— "How can a child of mine have no sense of direction?" her father fumed—but she excelled at cooking and art. It was clear to everyone, by the time the girls were in high school, that Sarah was "the creative one."

It is her father's fault that Sarah became an art teacher. He was the one who taught her to love art. He took Sarah and Abby to all the museums in Washington D.C., to natural history museums where they gaped at dinosaur skeletons and to art galleries where they stood in room after room hung with paintings, clasping their father's hand while he explained "what the artist was trying to show us." As a little girl, Sarah stood uncomprehending, allowing his words to pour over her like a hymn in a language she did not yet fully understand.

Years afterwards, she remembers when she first saw Picasso, and of course the Impressionists. But most of all, she remembers the Alexander Calder mobile hanging at the National Gallery of Art. Its huge liquid red shapes were suspended in an open atrium high above her head, moving gently with the air, and in motion creating new shapes. Her father's face changed when he looked up at the mobile. His jaw softened and his eyes went wide, as if he had been given a great gift, something new and immeasurable.

Sarah tightens her own jaw and tries to banish the image of her father's face from her mind. Daddy had wanted her to become an artist.

He harbored for years the secret dream of having a daughter whose paintings would be on display at a museum or gallery someday, maybe even at the Metropolitan Museum of Art. It had been Sarah's dream, too, until graduate school. "Passable but not inspired work," her advisor had typed on her end-of-year evaluation. "Ms. Gershman lacks the passion and seriousness of purpose that we see in the truly best students."

Sarah didn't offer any real explanation to her parents for her decision to look for a teaching job rather than continuing on with her fine arts degree. She had already made the mistake—once—of asking for her father's assessment of her work. In her first semester of art school Sarah brought home her portfolio, a collection of abstract charcoal sketches and oil paintings that she was quite proud of. Her father had taken the portfolio and spread her work out on the dining room table before him, and then surveyed it in complete silence while Sarah watched, nervously, from the doorway. He separated her work into two piles, lifting each sheet of paper, studying it carefully before depositing it in one of the two piles. Then he delivered his verdict. "These I liked very much. They're very good. This one especially, it's very powerful. These," gesturing dismissively to the second pile, "didn't speak to me." He stood up then, without looking at Sarah, and went to the refrigerator for a Pepsi. It became one of those signature events in her relationship with her father, the one that brought gasps of indignation from her friends years later, when she turned it into an amusing anecdote. And yet Sarah understood and was secretly envious of the impulse that allowed her father to judge so cleanly, to divide the world into worthy and unworthy, the mediocre and the Truly Best.

She could use some of that discernment now, Sarah thinks with a sigh, as she faces the tabletop full of student projects. The students' final assignment was to create a landscape, depicting either their favorite place or an imaginary one. The second and third-graders did simple oil pastel drawings, but in fourth and fifth grades Sarah introduces more complexity, allowing her students to choose from a variety of media. There are seascapes, moonscapes and cityscapes sculpted from clay, balsa wood, toothpicks, and Styrofoam; charcoal sketches and tempera paintings; and several cut-paper collages. The one she is struggling with the most is Maddie Russell's. Maddie is a quiet girl in second grade whose mother is dying of cancer. All the teachers love Maddie; the school secretary takes special care to say hello to her each morning when she trudges slowly by the front desk with her backpack. At lunchtime, when the other students avoid Maddie, not sure what to say, she eats at the teacher's table, often sitting beside Sarah and picking at her sandwich, not saying much.

Maddie adores art class, and enters into her projects with an intensity and focus that is unusual for her age. She worked on the final assignment for two weeks, drawing her practice sketches so feverishly and with such complete absorption during class that she often missed the end-of-class bell entirely.

Sarah expected Maddie's work to be good, but she is surprised to be so moved by the picture that the girl has created. It is a skillful drawing of a storm on the Chesapeake Bay, the water heaving and crashing against a rocky shore. Two birds are flying against the wind, trying bravely to reach their nest. At one edge of the drawing the waves have parted, and Maddie drew the figure of a woman, slender and solitary, making her way from shore deep into the parted waters. She seems to float just above the water with her face turned slightly away from the shore, moving toward a dark, threatening horizon. It is impossible to miss the sense of loneliness and danger that is alive in the little girl's picture of a mother disappearing into dark waters, leaving everyone behind.

The knock on the classroom door is so soft that Sarah almost doesn't hear it. "Ms. Bowers?" A man walks into her classroom. He is tall, with thick brown hair, and looks vaguely familiar, a parent she must have met on Back to School Night.

"I'm Tom Russell, Maddie's father," the man says. Sarah is so startled that her mind is nearly washed clean, and she cannot think of anything for more than a second. Then she manages to hold out her hand. "That's so strange," she says. "I was just looking at this when you came in. It's Maddie's. You should take a look, it's really very good."

Tom takes the sketch in his hands. He is a very large man, with broad shoulders that pull at his rumpled corduroy shirt. Sarah feels his pain like a presence in the classroom with them, expanding and contracting with their breathing. "I'm sure you know Maddie's mother is very sick," he says. "We're not sure how much longer she has. Maddie's having a very hard time."

"I'm so sorry about your wife. It's cancer?" Sarah asks, knowing the answer before he nods. If she closed her eyes, she knows she would see it, a burnt orange color like her father's cancer, raging and feral.

"God, I'm so sorry. I know—I mean, my father has cancer, too. Of the esophagus."

"Ovarian." Tom says, and despite herself Sarah feels a smile beginning. He is staring at her, and she feels like an idiot. "Oh, no," she apologizes again, "I'm sorry, it's just that everybody—we always seem to need to compare tragedies, you know? When you tell someone a loved one is dying of cancer, everybody's cancer stories come out of the woodwork. I didn't mean to suggest that I know what you're going through..."

Tom nods slightly. "You know Mr. Carmody, the janitor? His wife died of ovarian cancer last year. He tells me all about it every time he sees me."

"I had no idea about his wife," Sarah says. "You know Rose in the front office?"

"The one with the fabulous hats, right?" Tom asks. Miss Rose, as the kids call her, wears a different hat every day. Sometimes they are festooned with feathers or artificial roses, other days, a dragon or the Cat In The Hat. Zach's favorite one is the leprechaun hat she wore on St. Patrick's Day.

"Breast cancer," Sarah explains. "That's what started her wearing the hats. She's been doing chemo since Christmas."

"My wife hasn't lost much of her hair," Tom says. "I guess she's lucky." Almost without intending to, Sarah begins to confide in him, telling him about her father losing Zach in the toy store, and her dreams. They talk about Maddie and her mother, about the little girl's obvious gift for art, about luck and impermanence.

"I can't eat anymore," Sarah blurts out, and Tom gives her an odd look. It is not the look of someone who thinks she is crazy, but a penetrating, assessing look. When she explains—her loss of any physical desire, her appetites shut down—he nods, taking her completely seriously.

"It's the fear of what might happen," Tom says, "And not knowing when it will hit. You see it sometimes with victims of earthquakes or tornadoes, anyone who has had a huge shock."

Now it is Sarah's turn to give him a quizzical look.

"I'm trained as a first responder," Tom explains. "They call us out to help in emergency rescue situations. I haven't done it much in the past few years, since Maddie was born and Lily got sick; but I used to be called out two, maybe three times a year. They teach you basic first aid, stuff like that—but the most important things I learned were about PTSD, the emotional impact of a crisis. Sometimes that's as bad as the physical damage."

There are tangible manifestations of stress that can be treated medically, Tom continues to explain. Headaches, dizziness, sleep disorders, heart palpitations. Loss of appetite is common. But most of those symptoms flow from a mind and heart in distress, a wounded psyche that could not find peace. "I've seen men who survived an earthquake," he says, "A big one, 8.5 on the Richter scale. One guy, we pulled him out of an office building that collapsed around him, and it's a miracle he wasn't hurt at all, just a few cuts and scrapes. But afterwards he couldn't stand the sound of a spoon rattling against a teacup. He was always just waiting for the next bad thing to hit."

That's me, Sarah realizes. I'm fine except I'm always waiting for the ground to give way under my feet.

When the time comes for Sarah to pick Zach up from after-care and she thanks Tom for coming by, he invites her to spend an afternoon with him and Maddie sometime on his boat. It is only after Sarah and Zach are driving home that she realizes she has no idea why Tom had come to her classroom in the first place.

Maddie's drawing is still haunting Sarah that evening, as she sits outside on the back patio with Ginna, sipping wine and swatting mosquitoes. Zach is in bed, and Row has left the two women alone to talk. Connie stretches out at Sarah's feet on the cool grass, belly turned expectantly up, his nose burying happily in the dirt. It is one of those rare nights when calm has settled over the house, and contentment seems possible.

And yet Sarah cannot get Maddie's drawing, and her conversation with Tom, out of her head. She is thinking of the things that are precious to us and only ours, and how utterly they are gone from this world when we die. She tells Ginna about Tom coming into her classroom, all the while picturing his weary face, his confusion about what remains of the life he had known.

"I think a lot, these days, about what will be left behind when I go, you know," Sarah says into the soft air between them. "And all I can come up with is Zach. Zach will be here, however screwed up and unhappy he's going to be, he'll be walking around on this earth when I'm gone. And I guess maybe grandkids. It just doesn't seem like enough, you know?"

"You don't know how lucky you are." The heat in Ginna's voice stuns them both. "At least you have somebody…" She stops herself, twisting her bottom lip. "Oh, for Christ's sake." Ginna is a Catholic and rarely swears, and the words stumble out of her mouth.

"What?"

Ginna has had three glasses of wine, and her face has the crumpled look of someone who is not exactly sure of herself, who is trying to hang on to her composure. "It's just—you're not the only person on earth who has ever lost someone."

Sarah racks her brain to figure out what her friend is talking about. Both of Ginna's parents were alive and healthy the last time Sarah saw them, at their Christmas party.

"Ginna, what the hell?"

"I had a baby." Ginna says abruptly, her eyes avoiding Sarah's. "I was pregnant, and I lost her."

"Oh, my God." Sarah reaches for her friend's hand and holds it, stroking over the rough skin on Ginna's palm, feeling the deepening blackness of the night around them like a roaring in the pit of her stomach.

"Her name was Lainey. Short for Elaine. As soon as they said I was having a girl, I knew what I was going to call her. It was my grandmother's name."

In all the time she has known Ginna, her friend has never talked about a daughter. Sarah always assumed that Ginna and Pat couldn't have kids, that there was a simple and absolute verdict to explain their childlessness. She recalls now the rich silences that fall between them at times when Zach is around. Row had caught one of those moments on videotape once, sweeping the camera around the dining room table at

Zach's 2nd birthday party. The tape reveals Ginna watching as Zach pushes a plastic figure of Big Bird down through the white frosting of his cake with a toddler's deliberate glee, four plump fingers plunged into the cake, his face rapt—and then Ginna glances across the table, her eyes searching for Pat's with an earnestness that is so naked it melts into embarrassment as soon as her husband meets her gaze. Sarah sees a new melancholy in this scene now, recognizes the ache that lies beneath Ginna's kindness toward Zach.

"I lost her in my fifth month." Ginna says. "It was just one of those things."

Sarah knows that if she had lost Zach after five months of carrying him she would have crawled into the deepest hole she could find and might never have come out. She wants to tell Ginna how deeply Zach loves her, how much she means to their entire family, but she is unable to make a sound.

"She was a real kicker, too," Ginna continues quietly. "I couldn't sleep at all afterwards, because nothing felt right. I was so used to her kicking me in the ribs every night."

Sarah thinks, we will sit here for awhile and then we will pour some more wine, go inside and join our husbands, and this moment will be completely gone. And still she lets the time move by without trying to give it words, holding her friend's hand in her own, recognizing how pain blossoms silently, invisibly, in places where we don't expect to encounter it. She thinks of earthquakes and of cold evening rains, of a woman floating alone on turbulent blue waters, of shutters that slam shut in our hearts and then blow open in the thick of a storm, surprising us again and again.

Stan

The doctors don't know anything, Stan thinks to himself with great satisfaction. They didn't know why he got the cancer in the first place, and now they can't explain why it has receded so dramatically. "We haven't isolated a specific cause for cancer the way we have for many other diseases," his oncologist explains carefully. "Does smoking cause cancer? Yes and no. Some people can smoke two packs a day for forty years and never get cancer. We don't really understand what makes some people's cells decide to grow abnormally." The doctor smiles almost apologetically at Stan, palms thrown open as if to say, *Who knows?* "Back when I was in medical school we used to talk about cancer as an ordinary cell gone Bolshevik."

Stan's cells, it appears, are not inclined toward Communism. His tumors have nearly disappeared after six weeks of vigorous radiation, and his voice is returning. Well, it is not actually his original voice that he has retrieved—this is a different, deeper, more guttural dialect that has emerged, pressing itself up insistently through his former speech, with the stealth and mystery of a submarine. But Stan is more than happy to call it his. Even the speech therapist and the surgeon are amazed at how rapidly Stan has taught his mouth to form sounds. The muscle tissue they implanted to replace his tongue doesn't behave like an actual tongue; it is slower to respond to his brain's instructions, and there are some sounds—like a "th" or "sw," both of which require exquisite coordination of lips, tongue and teeth—that elude him completely. But the ability to make sounds at all, Stan has discovered, is a tremendous relief. When he first came home from the hospital and couldn't produce more than a growl, he fell silent. He thought he would never make a noise again, rather than sound like a wild animal. But after a few days of communicating only in brief notes scribbled on paper, the enforced silence began to drive him crazy. The need to produce meaningful sound, to communicate his thoughts and desires, became almost overwhelming.

Stan no longer has the sensation that his head will explode from the backup in his mental plumbing. He has even begun to imagine entire sentences that he will soon be able to deliver through his mouth. What a luxury to proclaim an entire sentence out loud, instead of confining himself to choppy abbreviations. His truncated thoughts are recorded on small pieces of paper all over the apartment and on tables and desks throughout his law office: *Hot. Cold. Pencil. Store? Need TP. Depo Mrs. Harkness.* It's not just laziness or haste that makes him write such short notes, it's Stan's impatience with the process. By the time he has scribbled an entire sentence and someone else has read and understood it, Stan has moved on; his brain is at least three sentences ahead. How astounding to be able to keep up with the normal pace of a conversation again. Although the therapist warns him not to get ahead of himself, not to expect too much. Next comes a round of chemo, to take care of any lingering cancer cells.

He needs to talk to Sarah. Every time he brings it up, Lynda tells him—like his physical therapist—that he is expecting too much, that he should give his daughter some time. They haven't communicated since the toy store episode with Zach. When Lynda calls, translating for him, Sarah is polite, as if she's talking to her distant cousin, twice removed. Stan announced that they were planning a visit on Saturday, scribbling to Lynda, "Coming to see you and Zach!" and Sarah said she was sorry, but this weekend wouldn't work out. She is behaving like a spoiled brat, depriving him of his own grandson.

The young woman who gets speech therapy at the same time Stan does is about Sarah's age, late thirtyish, with spiky red hair. She has cancer in her thyroid and salivary glands. They have acknowledged each other mainly with smiles and waves. Her name is Zinnia. Ordinarily, Stan would find this irritating—who names a child after a flower, really?—but he has allowed himself to be charmed by her. "Friends call me Zee," she explained when they met at Stan's first therapy session, and he felt a foolish little rush at the thought of being included among her friends.

Z, however, is one of the letters that Stan's mouth simply refuses to produce. Pronouncing this letter requires intricate coordination of palate, tongue and teeth that escapes him, no matter how much he practices.

Today, while he is resting in between sets of "La la la la las," Stan waves to get Zee's attention and manages to say something that approximates, "How's it going?"

She shrugs, an eloquent shrug that Stan interprets to mean: OK, I guess, some days are shitty and others are better. He nods his understanding, reaches for his notebook and scrawls, "What did U want to be when U grew up?"

This time the young woman's eyebrows fly up and she stares off into the room for a moment, taking his question seriously. Then she reaches for the notebook and writes, "Vet. But pre-vet = way too hard."

Stan thinks of Abby reading James Herriott's *The Bright and the Beautiful* and vowing, for one year, that she would become a vet. "Every girl's fantasy—to heal animals," he writes.

She is still taking him completely seriously, and thinks again for a while before answering. "Maybe, take nature & improve on it." Stan isn't sure what she means, writes a big question mark.

"In nature, animal gets sick, it dies, in pain. We change that."

Stan gestures to the room they're sitting in, shakes his head vigorously. "Sometimes Yes, sometimes No." Then he writes: "What job now?"

"School dietician. Decide which fruits & veggies your kids eat."

"So tell me, Is ketchup a vegetable?" Stan jokes.

Finally, a smile. "Have to be President of the U.S. to decide that."

He wishes he could still get a smile from his own daughters that easily. His last real conversation with Sarah, before he lost his voice, had been a disaster. It was after dinner at the Palm, and they were sitting, sipping coffee, Stan's with a generous shot of Grand Marnier.

"How are things with Row?" he had asked her. He watched three emotions move across his daughter's face: surprise, guilt, anger. She shrugged it off, but it left Stan wondering. "OK."

"Row is good for you, Sarah. Don't screw it up."

"Thanks for the vote of confidence."

"I'm just saying, recognize what you have. Row is your anchor. That's more important than you think."

"Says the man who's on Wife Number Three."

"Are you fighting?"

"Jesus, Dad, when you and Mom were together it was like the Battle of Midway every day at breakfast. Since when is it such a big deal to fight?"

Something in her tone made Stan uneasy, and he looked at her sharply. "Are you having an affair?"

"Talk about projection!" Sarah said hotly, but didn't meet his eyes.

"What does that—never mind, are you?"

Sarah nearly jumped up from the table. "Enough, Dad, stop with the Inquisition. If I were having an affair—which I'm not—it wouldn't be any of your business." She sounded shrill and insecure. A waiter hovered discreetly near their table, and Stan motioned silently for the check.

He no longer understands what makes his youngest daughter tick. He thought he knew her so well, when she was a girl, but Sarah as an adult, a wife and mother, baffles him completely. She is anxious all the time, she eats oddly, she no longer seems happy with her husband. Most important, she has given up her art. He loved Sarah's drawings, especially the ones she did in high school art class, so fluid and confident. There is one charcoal sketch Sarah made, of a female dancer, that Stan still swears to God could pass for a Degas. He had the sketch framed, and it hangs in the small study next to his bedroom. Sarah could have been somebody. Both of his daughters had talent—Abby had always loved music, and she had played the cello for years, and was not half bad. But Sarah had something special, Stan has always believed that.

What she does with stones, he doesn't understand that. My daughter hauls rocks from creeks and piles them up around her yard. That's art? Art, in Stan's mind, is creating something from nothing, taking the raw materials that nature provides—marble, oil, pigments, ash—and transforming them, conceiving something new. If Sarah carried the rocks back to her studio and chiseled and sculpted them down into new shapes, Stan could appreciate that. Wrestling meaning from nature, that's what art is supposed to be. Stan sighs. If he tried to teach his daughters anything, it was that you had to wrestle with life.

Sarah

Sarah gets five phone calls on her birthday. Her mother always calls her early in the morning to say Happy Birthday at exactly 7:25 a.m., the time that Sarah was born. The second and third calls are from Ginna and Helene. Hen calls next, and after wishing Sarah all the happiness in the world, she demands, "Do you have a good eye cream?"

Sarah is confused. "You need me to bring you eye cream?"

"No, not me." Hen says impatiently. "You need a good eye cream. Use it every night. A woman your age can't be too careful about those little tiny lines around your eyes."

Sarah promises to buy some eye cream, and hangs up. When the phone rings again an hour later, she is unprepared for the voice at the other end. "Hay, Jhwee-har'. Habby Bir-jhay."

"Daddy!" Sarah's entire body halts in mid-air. She is barely aware of walking as she carries the telephone over to the kitchen table and sinks down in front of the window.

"Yeh." He can't pronounce the final consonants in most words. His voice is growly and indistinct, without the exact timbre and richness that she knows. But it is undeniably the voice of her father. The sound brings a rush of sensations along with it—she can almost smell the Lucky Strikes in his front pocket, the tang of Old Spice on his face.

As a new mother, Sarah used to imagine being confronted with a roomful of hundreds of babies, all dressed alike, and having to identify her infant son. How would she know him? Don't all babies have the same cottage-cheese smell, don't they all spit a little when they laugh? She wasn't sure what the clues would be, but she had no doubt that on some deep sensory level she would recognize Zach, that her entire body would lean toward him like a plant urgent for light. The way her body bends now into the phone.

Her father has been seeing a speech therapist, has been fitted with a new prosthesis that allows his reconstructed tongue to form words. He worked with the therapist several days each week, Lynda explains, learning to force air up through his throat, enough to carry sound from his mouth, his lips mastering the shape of each letter all over again. "I can't believe it! You sound wonderful." Sarah keeps saying over and over.

Her father manages four sentences, and then Lynda takes over. They make plans for Sarah and Zach to visit soon. When Sarah hangs up the phone she stands motionless in her kitchen. Row has placed vases of white peonies—her favorite—in every room, and their sugary fragrance floats in the air. Everything floats for a moment, suspended by this thing she has not allowed herself to hope for.

When Abby and Sarah were younger, their father took them out to dinner each birthday to celebrate. He would choose the restaurant—usually a local steakhouse or Roma's for Italian food—and once the family was settled at the table and their drinks arrived, he would make a toast. It was the same every year. "I expect great things from you, sweetheart," he would announce, lifting his Bloody Mary with a broad smile.

Connie pads heavily over to where Sarah is standing in front of the window seat and looks up expectantly. Sarah sits down and pats the dog's head, hugging her knees to her chest. She stares out the window, then lifts her coffee mug in one hand. "I expect great things from you, Daddy," she says out loud.

Stan

S tan takes his coffee light, with two sugars. Sipping hot coffee is one of the pleasures that has been returned to him since his surgery. If he keeps a napkin under his chin to catch the drips, he can angle the cup carefully and pour the hot liquid into his mouth in sips that are small and manageable enough for him to swallow.

This morning he is on his second cup in the Royal Coffee Shop on Lexington Avenue, just down the street from the apartment building, thinking about his golf game. Last week, he had made it through nine holes at the club and almost shot his handicap. It's time to get Zach out on the putting green. If the boy starts early, he could really learn the game. He could really be somebody.

Earlier this morning he told Lynda he wanted to plan a trip to see the kids in Maryland. She gave him that "Mmm-hmmm" that really means No, we're too busy; or No, it's not a good time for a trip. Stan is still irritated, thinking about it. To avoid a fight, he had grabbed a sweatshirt and left the apartment, walking the two long blocks to his favorite coffee shop.

Stan stubbornly believes that it's possible to achieve harmony in his marriage. Three wives and two divorces should probably have taught him otherwise, but Stan is unwilling to be persuaded that things can't get better. He thinks of Lynda as his best wife yet. In fact, some days, he has no idea what he would do without her. But just as he never stops striving to improve his swing with a three-iron, refusing to accept that he has played his best golf game, Stan has never quite accepted that with his third marriage he might have achieved his personal best.

"Stanley!"

Only two people call Stan that: Wife Number One, and his former law partner, Dick Rozin. Stan looks up to see Dick striding through the door of the coffee shop. Dick's tailored grey silk suit and crisp cream-colored shirt make Stan keenly aware of his own rumpled state. He can't remember whether he'd bothered to shave this morning—or yesterday morning, either, for that matter—and here's Dick standing over the table, his partner's sharp eyes taking in the wads of damp paper napkin that litter the tabletop, the heap of empty sugar packets, Stan's stained yellow sweatshirt. Dick's eyes skim over these details and come to rest eagerly on Stan's face. "How are you, buddy?"

Stan's finger is already on his trach tube, his breath loud as he inhales deeply the way his speech therapist coached him to do, then propels the air up out of his chest and into his throat. "Kh-khant khomplh-lay." *Can't complain,* he wanted to say. Such an absurd amount of effort for a casual phrase—but Stan wants above all to appear casual.

He sees doubt flicker in Dick's eyes and knows his partner didn't understand him. Stan waves his hand, signaling that it doesn't matter, and looks around for his notepad. Dick is still standing over him, one palm flat on the table—a lawyer's courtroom stance—and Stan wishes he would sit down, for God's sake.

He finds the notepad, can't find his pen. Dick reaches into his jacket pocket and brings out a fountain pen—the same black and gold Parker pen Stan remembers he always used—and hands it to Stan.

How'd you find me? Stan scribbles, holding the page so Dick can see. This makes his partner smile.

"Leon." Dick says. Stan's doorman remembered Dick from the old days. "He told me where you'd be." Dick leans in close with a conspiratorial wink, close enough so that Stan can smell expensive aftershave, and can see the precise line of his partner's sideburns. He knows Dick has his hair cut every two weeks, at the same barbershop Stan used to go to. It looks like he's due for a trim.

"Oh, and don't worry," Dick continues, sliding finally into the booth across from Stan. "Your doorman won't let on to Lynda where you go every day."

The waitress pours coffee and Dick talks, launching into a summary of a complex workers' compensation case. This is the kind of case Stan and Dick had loved working on together: forcing businesses to be held accountable for the health and welfare of their employees. As long as he's talking, Dick is relaxed and expansive, his arms sweeping across the table for emphasis as he describes the particular challenges of the case. When he pauses and Stan reaches again for his notepad, Dick's arms fall to his sides.

Stan is scratching on his notepaper in the silence, feeling as if his head is about to explode. While Dick was talking Stan's thoughts were coming in rapid-fire succession, and he knows his hand will never keep pace with what he wants to say. He crosses out most of what he's written finally and scrawls the name of a case that relates to the issue his partner is working on.

Dick reads the note and mutely nods his appreciation, as if he too has somehow been reduced to sign language.

"How's Vivian?" Stan writes. He doesn't really care how Dick's batty wife is doing, but he needs badly to keep the conversation moving. He wishes he could take a sip of coffee, knows he will not attempt to navigate this in front of his partner.

Dick shrugs. "Vivian is teaching Tai Chi," he says, "and complaining that I work too much."

"So what else is new?" Stan scribbles with a smile. After a few more minutes of halting conversation, Dick glances around for the waitress and signals for the check.

"Keep the pen." Dick waves dismissively as Stan holds out the Parker. The wave bothers Stan. Who gives away a two-hundred dollar pen?

"NUH!" People at the next table turn to stare at Stan's guttural response. Stan's breathing is raspy and jagged, and he is fighting to control it. He can feel saliva pooling in the hollow space beneath his tongue, knows it is a matter of seconds before it runs from his mouth. Dick stands up, adjusting the lapels of his jacket, and looks at him almost beseechingly, his eyes saying, *Just let me do this, OK, buddy?* He leans down and gives Stan a quick, businesslike hug before he turns to go.

Part Two

Sarah

The brochure made the Sweetwater Monastery sound so inviting, a place of retreat and renewal nestled in the Shenandoah Valley. *Renewal is just what I need*, Sarah thought. *Yes*, and *Yes*, she had written emphatically on the application form, in the spaces where she was asked: Do you feel a need for quiet and inner peace in your life? And: Are you prepared to commit yourself to a challenging weekend of Zen practice?

Now she feels her neck muscles unknotting as she drives, Ginna in the passenger seat beside her, reading aloud the directions to a tiny mountain road forty miles above Winchester, Virginia, where the monastery sits high up on a hillside. They stop at a roadside coffeehouse for cappuccino—"Make them doubles, honey, we don't know when we're going to see another cappuccino," Ginna tells the young girl behind the counter—and then follow a narrow, bumpy gravel road up to the monastery.

The peace inside the dark, candlelit building is welcome, and the food in the dining hall is fresh and delicious. They are shown quietly to their room by a small, dark-haired woman in a white robe, where they find the hall bathroom and brush their teeth side by side at the sink, like schoolgirls.

"What's Pat doing this weekend?" Sarah asks as they pad down the hall toward their room.

"I think he's having a midlife crisis,"

"This weekend?" Sarah can't help herself, she is giggling.

"He wakes up in the middle of the night worrying that he's going to die, that he'll never reach sixty-five and be able to retire, that he won't leave me enough to pay the mortgage on the house and I'll have to move in with my brother." Ginna hates her brother. He lives in San Jose and vacations in the south of France and sounds to Sarah like he has a charmed life, but Ginna will have nothing to do with him.

"It's that turning sixty thing, right? It hits men hard sometimes." Sarah says sleepily.

Ginna sighs. "I know, I know. I'm trying to be understanding. I told him he can go buy a Corvette or pierce his nose or whatever he needs to do, just as long as he doesn't leave me for some sweet young thing." She plops down on the edge of her bed.

"He's an entomologist," Sarah points out. "Who would go out with him?" Ginna shoots her a dark look and climbs under the covers.

"He'll get over it, honey."

"I know, I know. Goodnight."

Sarah falls asleep Friday night feeling strangely calm. Row is taking Zach to his mother's house for the weekend, and there is absolutely no one who will need anything from her for the next forty-eight hours.

On Saturday the hours move slowly and thickly, but with purpose, from morning meditation at 4:45 a.m. to a nourishing breakfast, followed by a workshop on "Embracing Zen Practice." Sarah loves the time spent in the *zando*, the spacious, open meditation room in the center of the monastery's first floor. She is entranced by the faces of the monks, so gentle and forgiving, and the sound of their footfall soft on the worn wooden floorboards. *Really, I should spend more time around people like this,* Sarah marvels. She wonders whether Row and Zach would meditate with her, tries to picture the three of them lined up Buddha-like on their living room floor. She will need to rip up the living room carpeting, to see if there is a smooth hardwood floor underneath, like this one. Ginna is seated across from her, stretching the kinks out of her neck and wriggling to find a comfortable cross-legged position on the floor. Sarah closes her eyes and is content to sense the movement all around, the sounds of many bodies settling in, the monks swaying slowly above, silent and impassive as trees.

She is still not so sure about meditation. It intimidates her, the prospect of emptying her mind, letting all conscious thoughts spin away into dust and seeing only—what? the blank dark space beneath her eyelids? She tries to quiet her brain. Monkey mind, the monks call it, when your mind jumps from thought to thought, refusing to be still. *My father has cancer,* she thinks, and cancer cells bloom vividly in her imagination, travel at lightning speed through tissue and blood vessels, sparks of bright red against a thicket of black. This is exactly what happened to her when she joined that women's antiwar group to meditate for peace. They were all supposed to be conjuring images of light, love, and harmony, and all Sarah could visualize were tanks and charred bodies, orange bombs exploding. The women in the group were not too happy with her. She cannot, it seems, will herself to imagine something she does not believe in.

On Sunday morning, climbing out of bed for silent meditation at 6:00 a.m., Sarah's neck and shoulders ache from the unfamiliar pillow, or maybe from too much time spent meditating on a hard seat cushion. She is tired of being told when to wake up and when to lie down. She is especially weary of being told when she might speak and when to be silent. The gaze of the monks, which yesterday had seemed benevolent, in today's light is crisp and commanding, almost military. All those bald heads, she thinks, really get a bit monotonous. She fights the urge to tiptoe up to one of the senior monks and whisper in his ear. *My father has no tongue in his mouth,* she would confide. *What do you have to say about that?*

Her father is due for another MRI this week—just a look around to make sure things are still fine, Lynda had explained brightly on the phone. He did not come to the phone to talk to Sarah himself. Perhaps he, too, was having a difficult time believing in the improbable.

Sarah promises herself that she will not think about cancer during morning meditation. Instead, she stares dutifully at the head monk (uh-oh, now she is calling him Bald Head in her mind). She finds herself wondering, when she should be focusing on her breathing, if Baldy is aware of how overgrown his eyebrows have become. The thick black brows make him look extremely severe. It was the kind of thing you needed a wife or mother to tell you: time to trim your eyebrows, dear.

Morning meditation is followed on Sundays by breakfast (also in silence) and "Caretaking practice," a time when each participant performs a job for the good of the community: cleaning, gardening, clearing paths in the forest or removing trash. Sarah and Ginna are both assigned to cleaning the *zando*. Ginna, whose house routinely looks as if a hurricane had recently blown through, groans when the assignments are read, and stomps off to their room to change into work clothes. Sarah doesn't mind the job at all. In fact, she tells herself firmly, a good hour or two of cleaning in the *zando*—sweeping the broad wooden planks of the floor, tidying the seat cushions, a morning when her sole task is to usher in order where it is lacking—yes, that might be just the thing.

Nan, the intense, dark-eyed young woman who is in charge of the cleaning crew, meets them in the *zando*'s narrow entrance hall. The space is lined with wooden plank shelves for shoes, so that everyone enters the *zando* barefoot. Nan's feet are planted carefully side by side on the smooth wooden floor of the hall. She has a steady, sweet manner that Sarah finds soothing, but she can see that already the woman has set Ginna's teeth on edge. Nan describes the various cleaning tasks at length and with utter seriousness, as if she were discussing matters of state, and distributes brooms, mops and vacuum cleaners with an almost rapt attention. They are to mop with mindfulness, carefully sweeping their mops first in one direction and then the other in slow, curving arcs. When seat cushions are moved for cleaning, she explains in a hushed voice, they must be replaced in an exact, highly scripted manner.

Halfway through the morning, cleaning tasks are rotated. Nan comes up to Sarah where she is idly plumping the large cushions that sit at the head of the *zando*, the ones used by the senior Bald Heads. "Have you had a chance to vacuum yet?" Nan breathes, offering up a hand-held DustBuster in both arms.

"Uh, no, I guess not." Sarah is certain that when she receives the vacuum her face does not reflect the gratitude that Nan expects, because the young woman turns away quietly, her face downcast, her long ponytail swishing. Sarah remembers that Nan, when called by a monk yesterday to help with one of the rituals in the *zando*, fairly leapt into the air in her eagerness to serve, and rushed up the narrow aisle between the rows of cushions, her bare feet slapping on the floor.

It's a damned vacuum cleaner, Sarah mutters to herself, fiercely annoyed by the young woman's easy pleasure. The students at the monastery all seem to share an absorption in the minute movements of the day, a happiness with small things that is completely unrecognizable to her. It seems to her blind and simple, like the stupid joy of just-born kittens nuzzling their mother's belly and discovering milk.

She can't recall ever waking up feeling that particular kind of joy as a child, except maybe on her birthday. Nobody in her house was happy for long enough to really enjoy it. If something good happened, you turned it upside down and sideways, held it up to the light, examining every angle, searching for the catch that was always there. Anger, disappointment, those were familiar. A keen awareness—like a sharp unyielding lump in your side—of the unfairness of life, yes. But gratitude? Slowly moving her DustBuster over the crimson pillow covers along the east wall of the *zando*, Sarah concludes that gratitude was not built into her constitution.

"Maybe it's just not Jewish." Ginna offers later that afternoon. "Jews don't feel grateful. They kvetch." The two friends sit beside a small, sparkling creek on the hill overlooking the monastery, the roar of water driving away all conscious thought, until it becomes an effort to speak.

"Tell me what happened after—you know, when you lost the baby." Sarah says finally. Ginna is gazing into the creek and doesn't lift her eyes.

"What do you want to know?"

Sarah isn't sure. "Did you try again?"

Ginna shakes her head, so much sadness tugging at her face that Sarah wants to hug her. "I wanted to, but Pat wouldn't. And to be honest, I'm not sure I could have gone through that again, being pregnant and wondering every minute if the baby would be okay this time."

Sarah nods, and they sit in silence for a long time, the sunlight sliding lower and lower on the trunks of the trees that surround them. They have skipped afternoon meditation, and now are in danger of missing the evening meal as well, but Sarah doesn't care. She couldn't face a room full of Bald Heads and their disciples right now. In fact, she has no desire ever again to be in the company of people who are so sure—so simply and reverently sure—of the path ahead, as if it were not unthreading before their very eyes, as if the ground beneath all of our feet were not eroding faster and faster by the second.

"I want to go home," she says.

Reiju Sensai, the senior spiritual leader of the monastery, is not pleased that two of his weekend students are leaving the retreat early.

Sarah stands fixed by his penetrating disapproval, almost ready to relent and stay. "I have to go home," she explains suddenly, the lie coming easily in a burst of desperation. "My son is sick." The sensai seems to consider this. "How old is your son?" he asks quietly. Sarah takes a deep breath, prepares to answer. What was the right thing to say?

"Two." Ginna answers for her, lying with sunny confidence. Sarah shoots her a sideways look of admiration. Two is perfect. A two-year-old definitely still needs his mother when he is sick.

The sensai's bald head bobs slowly, shining above them in the small, crowded office. Sarah and Ginna endure a somber lecture about participating fully in their own spiritual enlightenment. Ten minutes later, finally, they are released. They pack their overnight bags and toss them into the car under the watchful eyes of several monks, and then they are peeling out of the gravel driveway in Sarah's car with the windows rolled down and the radio turned up full blast playing the Indigo Girls, feeling a little like Thelma and Louise. Sarah knows she is headed back to a tidal wave of obligations: doctor's appointments for Zach, dinners to cook, Row. She has successfully avoided thinking about her husband since they arrived. She trails her fingers out the window to feel the hot breath of wind and the car bumping along the road. *This*, she thinks, letting the air blow across her open palm, savoring the thrill of escape. *This one moment, this is mine.*

Stan

A crowd has gathered around the boy dancing on the sidewalk on the corner of Kosciuszko Street, attracted by his audacity. This kid is a skilled dancer, the muscles in his legs attesting to years of practice; and he moves with confidence to Donna Summer's "Hot Stuff," which booms from a speaker at his feet. But it is his outfit that is prompting smirks and admiring glances. Dressed in drag, this boy could be mistaken for a slimmer, teenaged version of Donna herself. Throwing his hips around with abandon, he makes his way through the crowd, blowing lascivious kisses to the men with a broad, lipsticked mouth.

"Work it, sister," a young man next to Stan calls out, swiveling his own hips. Stan is enjoying the spectacle, tapping out the beat of the music with one foot, until Lynda tugs on his sleeve.

She had been dead set against this trip—had, in fact, looked at him like he was crazy when he suggested coming all the way to Brooklyn this morning. The sky was overcast, threatening rain, and Lynda warned that they would get caught in a downpour. Stan counts it as a small personal triumph when he can convince his wife to do something she doesn't want to do. "Well, it's against my better

judgment," she grumbled as they boarded the Number 4 train, finding
the last two seats on the car next to a group of Chinese students with
overstuffed backpacks. I'm making this trip ALA, Stan tells himself
with secret relish. Against Lynda's Advice.

Now he glances over at his wife's face, lined with worry and
impatience, her cheeks flushed—had she put on makeup for this outing
to Brooklyn?—and waves her away. Stan is determined to prolong the
moment, to let Donna Summer drown out everything else. Lynda
smiles her resigned smile and tucks an arm through his, protectively.

Someone watching the two of them might find this charming,
the way they engage in small gestures and few words, an old married
couple finishing each other's sentences. The evidence of their
collaborative communication is everywhere in their apartment, in the
pages torn from Stan's notebooks, the scribbled phrases that cover
every table. Stan's notes by themselves are unintelligible, capturing only
his portion of a conversation. He scrawls comments about the day's
news headlines, a request for lunch, a complaint about his reading or
his stomach tube. "What happened in Japan!" "Car insurance?" "potato
salad." The rest of the conversation is filled in by Lynda's chatter, and
it seems to Stan that the less he says, the more his wife talks, her voice
ballooning, rising in the empty air and then settling deflated alongside
his inarticulate rasps, coughs, and gargles.

Stan refuses to acknowledge that he is diminished by his
illness; and yet now that he cannot verbally dominate every
conversation or even reliably muster the physical strength that he once
counted on, something has shifted between them. It's as if Lynda is
emboldened by his silence, and that is something that Stan simply

cannot have. Today's trip is his first step toward setting things right again, showing her that he is still firmly in command.

He is enjoying the smells of Brooklyn's streets, a pungent blend of cigarettes, perfume, pizza, and last night's garbage. He remembers, suddenly, the fragrance of tobacco and chocolate that would greet him when he entered the candy store on the corner of Kosciuszko and Throop. The enticing smile of the blonde-haired girl who worked behind the counter.

He motions to Lynda that he's ready to walk, ignoring the beginnings of a cramp in his leg. Stan is sure he'll be able to find his old house. Lafayette is a shady street lined with two-family row houses and modest apartment buildings, each one with a tiny patch of grass in front. Stan is surprised to see that most of the front lawns are well-tended and bursting with flowers. He had heard that the neighborhood was going downhill.

He stops to point out a four-story brick apartment building with a set of steep concrete steps. The steps, once lined with red geraniums, are surrounded now by bare dirt and a few scrappy patches of grass. "My Uncle Lou's house," Stan scribbles.

Uncle Lou lived alone, and he came over to Stan's house every week for Sunday dinner. "He showed me magic tricks when I was little. Pulled quarters out of my ear."

Lynda gives him a look, and Stan wonders why he'd told her that, of all the things he might have offered about his uncle. Uncle Lou was the one who encouraged Stan to consider becoming an architect. "Dream big, boys," he would say, one hand landing heavily on Stan's shoulder, making Stan squirm. Robbie was going to be a golf pro, which pleased their father, but Stan didn't know what he wanted to be. He had no idea what an architect did, really, but he did wish he could design a great building someday, or a structure as magnificent as the Brooklyn Bridge. Stan and Robbie rode their bikes down to the waterfront to gaze up at the taut steel cables of the bridge stretching overhead for what seemed like an impossible span across the East River. When Stan looked up at the huge arches of the bridge it was like being near the girl in the candy store—his heart seemed to pump faster, and he had a sudden taste of possibility, of a road unwinding before him, offering things he suspected he didn't deserve.

Stan knew that Uncle Lou's wife had died in a concentration camp. Nobody in the family ever spoke her name. The Holocaust was something that was deeply understood in this neighborhood, etched into its memory—whose family hadn't lost someone to the Nazis? And who didn't know it could happen again?—but never talked about. Stan was always a little afraid in Uncle Lou's apartment, as if hanging in the air was the gravity of all those deaths, the presence of an overwhelming force with the power to obliterate him.

Getting cancer, he realizes now, is like being a Jew in Nazi Germany. You are surrounded by something that wants you dead. What are you going to do? You either decide to fight, or you run and hide like Anne Frank. And we all know how well that worked out for her, Stan thinks.

He and Lynda agreed yesterday to take a break from talking about his illness—a cancer holiday—so Stan doesn't share these thoughts with his wife. Instead, he continues walking slowly down Lafayette Avenue to the middle of the block, and there it is: the house he grew up in, back when everything held together, before Robbie got sick.

Lynda gazes up at the old house with its broad front porch and brick façade, badly in need of re-pointing. The first-floor windows open into a small front room, the dining room and kitchen in back. Upstairs, the bedroom that Stan and Robbie shared had a window that faced out onto the street. The elm tree they used to climb, Stan sees, has been cut back so its branches no longer scrape against the house. The front room curtains, which used to be dark green, have been replaced by bamboo shades.

"It's very nice," Lynda says after a pause. "It must have been a lovely house back then." She looks expectantly at him then, signaling: well, it's done, can we go now? Stan is not certain what else he wants, but he knows it is more than this. He shakes his head, deflated but stubbornly refusing to give in.

There is a park a block away, where Stan and Lynda sit on a bench and watch the neighborhood. Stan listens to the dogs barking in the park and the sounds of clanging metal coming from Fleischman's plumbing and heating supply house on the corner, smells cheese and garlic drifting from the doorway of the pizza shop next door. Somewhere in the park a mother slaps her son, and the little boy begins to wail. Stan gets a sudden vivid picture of Mrs. Bea, his best friend George's mother, who kept a big wooden spoon hanging inside her kitchen cupboard for the sole purpose of swatting the boys whenever they misbehaved. On the frequent occasions when the spoon came out, Stan and George would turn and run full-speed up the stairs to George's bedroom, leaving his mother red-faced in the stairwell, shaking the spoon like a fist over her head. That's what's wrong with parents today, Stan believes: they don't know when their kids deserve a good swat. It's reassuring to know some parents aren't afraid to be parents. He sighs, feeling suddenly happy. The weight of this neighborhood's history, his history—Mrs. Bea and her wooden spoon, Uncle Lou's hand on his shoulder, the shadow of the Nazis and the smile of the candy-shop girl, dogs yipping and kids riding bikes under the soaring expanse of the Brooklyn Bridge—seems no longer burdensome but instead a buoy, capable of lifting Stan and protecting him, carrying him over the turbulent waters, up and away from danger.

Sarah

Sarah is curiously content at funerals. Everything seems as it should be – the weeping, the somber clothing, the quiet, hollow feeling of loss. The truth is out there, spilling on the floor for everyone to see: *Life ends. You can count on it.* Not the chemo drip, not the MRIs, not the Bald Heads or the tarot cards that her friend Helene always wants to throw for her. *Trust this.* As she searches for a seat at Lily Russell's funeral, Sarah feels lighter, unburdened by the pretense that everything is going to be just fine. She lets herself be soothed by the hushed church, the wooden pews rubbed soft by hundreds of congregants pressing themselves expectantly forward, Sunday after Sunday.

At the graveside service for her friend Danny, who died of AIDS twelve years ago, long before anyone was ready to lose him, Sarah had sobbed loudly, uncontrollably, during the entire service. It was raining, the heavy patter of the drops on the tent above them almost—but not quite—loud enough to hide her gasps. Even Danny's parents, hunched together in the front row of folding chairs, had turned their heads ever so slightly to see who was making such a fuss. Row, standing next to her, his loafers muddy in the wet, close-cropped grass, had seemed to shrink back from her. At the time Sarah had wanted to cry alone, had not wanted anyone to shush her. Now, though, she wonders why her husband hadn't moved to comfort her, feels the absence of his arm around her shoulders like the sharp pang of an old injury.

They had played "Corner of the Sky" at Danny's funeral, Sarah remembers, his favorite song from "Pippin," which had only made her cry harder. Danny and his lover had planned the entire service, had gone over it months ahead of time. It was a beautiful service. And so considerate, to plan ahead.

She has found a seat, settles herself comfortably next to a group of people from school. Rose is there, wearing a soft gray felt hat with a single white flower tucked tastefully above the brim. She seems to be sitting with the members of Lily's cancer survivors group, five women, each with a scarf or hat covering her head, their arms tucked around each other, sparkling with a fierce blend of protectiveness and pride. Their eyes are quiet, resigned; this is a death that everyone has been preparing for.

"Lily Russell," the minister intones, "Was a good woman. A loving wife and mother." Murmurs and nods from the crowd. Sarah's eyes scan the front of the church for Tom and Maddie. There they are, Tom's broad shoulders slumped forward, one arm wrapped around his daughter, his palm patting her elbow over and over again. Maddie's mouth is tight, her cheeks shining with a few slow tears.

Sarah goes back to the house briefly after the service. She finds Tom settled into a chair out on the narrow front porch, staring out into the fields below. Tom and Lily's house rests on a hill overlooking acres of farmland that dip into a deep stretch of woods at the bottom. The waters of the Chesapeake Bay lie somewhere down below, beyond the trees. An old tobacco barn still stands on the property, its slanted graying roof shining silver in the late afternoon sun. "Most of this will be Maddie's someday," Tom says in a blank voice. "Hell, I hope she wants it."

"This is your family's land?" Sarah asks.

Tom nods. "My grandfather's. He built the barn, to cure tobacco. Now it's mostly soybeans, you can't sell tobacco anymore."

Sarah reaches for his arm. She makes her voice sound firm. "Maddie will be fine," she says. "She's a strong little girl and she has a wonderful father." Tom nods, with a look on his face that says he does not believe it.

When Sarah was pregnant with Zach, before she could even sense that there was actually a baby growing inside her, she taped the printout from her first ultrasound onto the refrigerator. He was in there somewhere, a dot of white snow in that field of black, smaller than a Cheerio. Sarah awoke every morning imagining that she could hold her embryo in the palm of her hand all day long. She used to wish she could carry him with her from room to room—just the tiny speck of him—cupped in one hand, her fingers curled up ever so slightly to protect him. She would lay him gently on the kitchen counter while she made her morning decaf coffee and poured Frosted Flakes into a bowl. She would cover him with her hand when she had to sneeze so he wouldn't blow away. So tenderly, she would carry him. We're not able to give our children shelter for very long, she knew. Might as well start early.

The idea of private art lessons for Maddie comes to Sarah a few weeks later, as she is helping Ginna to train the unruly hedges in her front garden into the shape of a large dragon's tail. Ginna is famous in the neighborhood for her topiary creations. The first two were created unintentionally—a pair of matching English boxwoods that Ginna trimmed so unevenly, trying to round them into balls, that they ended up looking like lumpy teddy bears. From then on, the children waited expectantly each spring, to see what creatures Ginna's garden would yield. Over the years she has attempted Winnie the Pooh, a family of dinosaurs, and an enormous Clifford the Big Red Dog, at Zach's request. Clifford was sculpted from an overgrown laurel hedge and wore a big red ribbon around his neck at Christmas.

Today they are working on a large dragon, and Sarah is struggling to give shape to the tip of the tail, clipping away at the leaves with abandon. Ginna walks over and surveys her friend's work with a critical eye. "I thought you said you went to art school," she says. "This looks like the Abominable Snowman."

"Animals were never my strong point." Sarah protests. "Now, if you'd like a nice still life, a bowl of fruit, maybe, that I can do." She stretches her arms over her head, tilts her neck toward one shoulder and then the other. "Isn't it time for a break yet?" She drops her pruning shears and pulls off a pair of flowered suede gardening gloves. Because gardening is her passion, Ginna has a huge collection of gardening gloves in every imaginable color—striped, patterned and solids—all crammed into a big plastic bin inside the shed. She insists that her gloves suit her mood, and changes them frequently as she works.

"You know who would be good at this?" Sarah says thoughtfully. "Maddie Russell. She has a great imagination."

"The girl whose mother died?"

Sarah nods. "Yes! Gin, I don't know why I didn't think of this before. I could give her private tutoring in art, after school. She'd keep Zach company. He's been painting up a storm. And you could show her how to do topiary."

Ginna lays a hand on Sarah's shoulder. "You can't be her mother, honey."

Sarah just stares. "I've been meaning to clean up my studio out in the garage. It would be good for me to get out there again, too." *You didn't see her eyes at the funeral,* she is thinking. *That scrunched little face.*

Tom is glad to hear from her when she calls, the desolation palpable in his voice. It has been barely a month since the funeral, and nobody is calling. Maddie keeps to herself, tucked upstairs in her bedroom, where a framed photograph of her mother now hangs beside the bed. "Her aunt Kay, Lily's sister, has been helping out a lot," Tom explains, "But it would be wonderful for her to get out, be with other people." They make a date for the following Monday afternoon.

"Nobody knows what to say to a little girl who has just lost her mother," Sarah says softly. "Give people time. Her friends will call."

"It's like they're afraid it's catching," Tom says. His voice is not bitter, it is the opposite of bitter, rinsed clean of all emotion.

"I know," Sarah replies. She hates the frozen, deer-in-the-headlights looks she gets from acquaintances at school when she mentions that her father has cancer. Even the doorman in her father's building, who has known Sarah since she was in college, who asks how Mr. Gershman is doing every time she comes to visit, looked a little shaken the one time when Sarah answered truthfully. She had begun to describe the feeding tube that attached to a plastic nozzle in her father's stomach, how it clogged up sometimes, when she saw the expression on Leon's face and stopped. Nobody really wants to know, she had realized with a flash of embarrassment, waving her hand and making a dash for the elevators. They don't want to know.

Stan

"How's your wife?" Zee has scribbled this on a piece of paper, and Stan understands it to mean: How is your wife handling the cancer these days? Avoiding Zee's eyes, he shrugs. Zee and Lynda had met only once, when Lynda accompanied Stan to a speech therapy appointment, and they had sat together long enough for Zee to recognize how shaken Lynda was by her visit. The large speech pathology room is typically filled with a cacophony of sounds from the several patients undergoing treatment at any one time, which Stan now takes for granted, but which can be unnerving for a newcomer. Today, Zee sits in front of a computer screen practicing loud and emphatic "L" sounds: "I LIKE the LLAMA with the YELLOW COLLAR." She is making great progress; the speech pathologist said last week that Zee would be speaking fluently again in no time.

In another area of the room, separated from them only by a thin curtain, a three-year-old diagnosed with childhood apraxia is banging out a repetitive series of notes on a xylophone, and a middle-aged woman seated nearby is exhaling air loudly into a long tube designed to help her stop stuttering. At the end of each breath the woman inhales, reads aloud a string of words on the computer monitor in front of her, swings her arms high above her head, then breathes out noisily and starts the sequence over again.

The sounds are oddly comforting to Stan now; he takes them as evidence of progress, proof that calculated, persistent physical effort can triumph, sometimes, over the madness and irrationality of disease. But he is more comfortable here without Lynda watching, when he can talk—and yes, flirt a bit—with Zee.

"I LOVE the way you say LLAMA," he writes on a piece of notepaper, holding it up in front of her. Zee sputters a little in the middle of her sentence, laughing, and waves him away. Her responses are being timed by the computer, Stan knows, so he leaves her alone.

If Lynda were here, she would simply roll her eyes at him with her tolerant, I-suffer-all smile. The fact is that when he married Lynda he chose someone who he might fail again and again, but who will never turn her back on him. She was his safe girl, the one who he could be sure wouldn't get away. Stan still doesn't understand why his first marriage failed. He came home for dinner one night to find Evie sitting at the kitchen table with a suitcase and two shopping bags at her feet. The specifics of this memory always troubled Stan. When had Evelyn packed the suitcase—while the girls were downstairs, Abby practicing cello and Sarah watching TV? In his mind she took only one suitcase—the brown one with the green pom-poms on the handle that she always packed for their trips to Ocean City—but how could you possibly fit everything from fifteen years of marriage into one medium-sized brown suitcase?

His second wife left him for another man after only one year. An orthodontist, for God's sake. The thought of losing to a man who wraps braces around people's teeth for a living galls Stan, even more than the fact of having two ruptured marriages. He should never really have expected Megan to stay, he sees that now. She wanted someone who would buy her a house in Vail and an apartment in Paris, and Stan was never going to make that kind of money.

Lynda would never simply announce that she was moving in with an orthodontist, Stan is completely confident of that. Even if she wasn't devoted to him, Stan has a trump card now: cancer. One way or another, they were going to survive this thing together. That ought to bring him comfort, he knows, but instead it floods him with unease. Run away, he wants to tell his wife some days. Go now, before it gets worse. When he woke up this morning and saw an empty space in the bed next to him he felt only a rush of relief, until he heard the sounds of Lynda making tea in the kitchen, preparing for another day.

Stan is waiting for his MRI results. He tries to explain this to Zee, manages to gargle out: "Emmou- wi" before becoming impatient and reaching for his pen and pad. "MRI results today."

Zee reaches out to squeeze his hand, her face full of hope. Stan scribbles on the pad again: "Feeling it's going to be good news." She nods with a big smile and Stan smiles back, pleased at his ability to make Zee believe in him.

Words on the page, those are Stan's most trusted tools. He can persuade anyone of anything with the right turn of phrase. He knows the hidden power of language, the way a string of letters can rain down on a person with the force of a blow, can reduce a strong man to tears or lift him with joy. He turns back to his task—repeating a series of two-syllable words with "R" in the middle—with renewed vigor. *Carrot, Hurry, Partner.*

Zee nods encouragement as Stan turns to go at the end of his session, giving him one of her beautiful, beaming smiles. Sunlight streams in from the window behind her, making her many silver earrings sparkle and creating a glow around her spiky orange-tinted hair so that she appears to Stan like a gothic angel embedded in the glass. His angel. Zee lets out a stream of gurgles and grunts that Stan understands means: "Good luck!" He waves in a way he hopes appears jaunty and light-hearted, and heads out the door.

Sarah

The phone call comes when Zach is talking about his favorite dinosaur, the micropachycephalosaurus, which lived during the late Cretaceous period and grew to be no more than two feet long. Sarah almost misses the ringing of the phone because Zach is repeating the name over and over, at full volume, captivated by the sound of the mounting syllables: "MI-cro- PA-chy- CE-pha-lo- SAU-rus!"

Sarah is standing at the kitchen counter, trying to decide whether to put in canned peaches or applesauce with Zach's peanut-butter and honey sandwich. She listens to Lynda's strained voice, her father's raspy breathing on the other extension. The cancer is back. The MRI didn't show anything, but her father's complaints about soreness in his mouth prompted another series of tests, and yesterday there they were: two small growths, one taking hold in the back of his throat, and the other one on the underside of his mouth.

They talk for a few moments, quietly, about chemotherapy, pain medication, which doctors to consult next, until Sarah's head feels like it has lifted off her neck and is in danger of blowing through the roof. Hanging up the phone, she turns wordlessly back to the kitchen counter, to the plastic Tupperware container full of snack foods for her son's lunch.

She stares for a minute and then shoves aside the canned peaches, reaches instead for a large bag of Chips Ahoy cookies. Ripping the bag open, she begins pouring cookies in a furious avalanche into Zach's open lunchbox. She heaps in so many cookies that she buries his peanut butter sandwich and his box of Juicy Juice, and then pours in more, until the velcro closure on the lunchbox almost will not shut.

The phone rings again. She has been waiting for a week for an appointment with the principal of Zach's new elementary school, and now the woman decides to call her back. Could she come in this morning at eleven? Why not?

Sarah drives Zach to summer camp in silence, grateful for once that he seems preoccupied and is staring out the window for most of the fifteen-minute ride. She walks him to the door and squeezes his hand—their private signal, since Zach will no longer tolerate public kisses—and whispers, "Have a great day, sweet boy. I love you." When his small body disappears inside the building, she fights the urge to run inside and grab him, so she will not be left standing alone in a busy parking lot, with absolutely no idea what to do.

Forty minutes later, she is, instead, seated across from Lavinia Merkin, the principal of Hunting Creek Elementary school, describing her son. His daydreaming, his boundless imagination, the way he memorizes countless details about dinosaurs, his propensity to forget the task he is supposed to be working on. "He needs a teacher who will really understand him and keep him on track," Sarah concludes. "I'm concerned that he might get lost in kindergarten. From what I've seen, Ms. Verde's class would be excellent for Zach." Sarah had sat in on Caroline Verde's kindergarten class, and admired the way the young woman moved around the room, keeping a watchful eye on each of her students in turn, gently separating two boys who were irritating each other, touching the arm of a little girl who missed her mother. She was animated and funny, able to keep the dullest child's thoughts from wandering.

"We find that many children have issues with the transition from preschool to kindergarten," Mrs. Merkin says soothingly. "I have three kindergarten teachers, and they are all very skilled at helping your child to make that transition an easy one."

Helene and the other teachers had warned her that she would get nowhere with Lavinia Merkin. Lavinia is the kind of principal who does not welcome too much parental involvement in her school, especially from teachers. Sarah takes a breath and tries again. "No, I've handled transition problems with kids in some of my own classes," she begins, "and this is different. Zach truly gets lost to the world for a while—it's as if he goes away."

"Have you considered the possibility that he is having seizures?" Lavinia asks sweetly. "What you're describing sounds quite a lot like a petit mal seizure."

"What?" Sarah pictures Zach lying in a white hospital bed, electrodes attached to his shiny, scrubbed scalp while a machine tracks his brain waves. The little bit that Sarah knows about epilepsy does not seem to apply at all to her son. "He just spaces out," she explains, "I can usually bring him back by touching his shoulder. He definitely needs a teacher who can help him to stay focused."

She is repeating herself, and the look of fixed compassion on the principal's face is beginning to seem condescending. This woman is seriously getting on her nerves. Lavinia clears her throat. "I would suggest that you consult with your pediatrician," she says, "An EEG can tell very quickly if there's any seizure activity, you know. There are other neurological disorders you might want to rule out as well. Petit mal seizures are very easy to control these days with medication. We have two third graders with epilepsy, in fact, who are doing just fine. We can, of course, come up with an IEP for Zachary as soon as we know what the diagnosis is." Sarah hates the sound of her son's name in Lavinia's mouth. She is aware that IEP stands for Individualized Educational Plan, a requirement before any public school child with special needs can receive different treatment in the classroom.

I just want Miss Verde for my son's kindergarten teacher, Sarah wants to scream. Her hands rub together uselessly under the table, the thumbs smoothing the undersides of her index fingers again and again. She is no longer listening to the stream of words coming towards her. She is, without warning, standing up and fumbling for her purse, and to her horror, tears have begun running down her face.

"Thank you," she mutters, noticing the principal's startled look and figuring that she must have interrupted Lavinia in mid-sentence. Sarah wipes her wet face hastily with the back of one hand, grabs her purse and notepad and starts for the door.

"Oh, my dear." Lavinia is, inexplicably, crooning. She tries to hug Sarah, folding her into an awkward embrace and patting the back of her shoulders with a warm, heavy hand, the nubby fabric of her jacket sleeves scratching unpleasantly against Sarah's neck. Sarah is deeply afraid that she will hit this woman if she doesn't let go immediately. She manages to wrestle herself free without, she hopes, appearing too ungrateful.

Outside, in the safety of the school parking lot, Sarah takes several deep breaths to calm herself and reaches for her cell phone. Tom Russell answers on the third ring. "Can I take you up on your offer of a boat ride?" Sarah blurts out. If Tom is taken aback by the abruptness of her request, he doesn't show it. He sounds delighted to hear from her, in fact, insisting that it will be no trouble at all. He has just returned from the morning's fishing trip and is free for the afternoon. He asks Sarah to meet them at the marina in two hours.

Sarah will have just enough time to pick Zach up from camp and stop at the grocery store for a few things. She will pack a lunch, she decides, a way of saying thank you for the boat ride that is fast becoming her salvation on this humid summer afternoon, the only thing that can carry her away from stubborn school principals and hospital schedules and diagnoses.

"You've been on a boat before," Tom is watching Sarah settle herself comfortably next to Zach on the outside deck of his boat, the "Lily Pad." "You know how to move around on one."

Sarah nods. "My father built Sunfishes when I was little."

In the cramped garage of their house in the suburbs, her father hammered together trim twenty-two-foot sailboats, constructing them diligently from handyman's kits that arrived in the mail. He built three of them over the years, and each time it was the same. First, the instructions would be spread out on the dining room table for a week or two while he studied them, copied down lists of materials to buy, and argued with his wife about how the boat should be put together. Sarah accompanied him to the local Hechinger's hardware store, breathing in the mingled smells of sawdust, paint and sweat as she held her father's hand.

Then her father disappeared into the garage, working late into the night after work and on the weekends, the whine of his table saw and the sounds of his outraged "Goddammit to hell!" whenever something didn't fit exactly right, drifting back toward the house where the girls lay trying to sleep.

For the first boat, Sarah and Abby's mother had helped to make the sail. She stitched the seams on an old Singer sewing machine that the girls rarely saw her use, her hands tight with determination, billows of stiff white fabric surrounding her at the kitchen table. The girls were filled with awe, watching the big needle dip in and out of the sailcloth, noticing that their mother was smiling now and then as she worked. Humming, even. After the boat was finished, though, she quickly lost interest. She started inventing excuses when their father wanted to take the family out on the boat, and he would end up hooking up the boat trailer by himself and leaving the house silently with Sarah and Abby. There was a permanent groove cut in the grass at the bottom of their driveway, where the wheels of the boat trailer ran onto the lawn and Daddy cursed and swung the steering wheel hard to the left, narrowly missing the mailbox each time.

Out on the water, the Patuxent River spreading out in shining ripples of light, the boat slapping up and down on the waves, Sarah felt that the world had suddenly breathed itself open before her. She knew she could exist here, wide-eyed and wide-hearted, forever. Her father felt this way, too, or at least Sarah believed that he did. He always wore a look of mild astonishment on the boat, as if, Sarah thought, he was remembering something wonderful that he couldn't believe he had forgotten.

Despite their father's best efforts, neither Sarah nor Abby ever learned much about sailing. More than once the huge sail coming about would knock one of the girls into the water, and Daddy would have to help her climb back onto the slippery wooden deck, sunburnt and sputtering. More often than not, the boat was swamped in the long creek that led from their neighborhood dock out to the river, and they found themselves paddling it, "more like a raft than a sailboat, really," as Lynda had remarked demurely on her first journey aboard. The Sunfish never floated well, actually; it rode only two or three inches above the water surface, and water cascaded over the deck at the slightest swell. And yet their father remained undaunted by these challenges, by lackluster winds and slack sails and his disappointed children, as if the next perfect sailing day still waited for them, always just around the corner.

Whenever Sarah finds herself on a boat, she falls into the easy rhythm of those childhood days, staring dreamily out over the water. She is aware, each time, of how her own breathing is muffled by the sounds of the water sloshing up against the sides of the boat, the salty spray clinging in a fine mist to her eyelashes and hair. It is the feeling of being carried that she loves best, being conveyed from one place to another without a single drop of effort on her part. She can remember her father asking, "Don't you want to learn how to sail it yourself?" and hears herself thinking no, that's not the point at all.

Tom is steering the boat, his back to Sarah, so that she can admire his tanned shoulders and the muscles that tighten under his white tee-shirt without embarrassment. *He has that outdoorsy look that gets to me,* she imagines explaining to Ginna. *He steers like a man who knows where he is going.* She can see Ginna rolling her eyes.

"My husband doesn't like boats," she finds herself confiding to Tom. "Well, it's not that he dislikes them so much, he mistrusts them, doesn't feel safe. He nearly drowned once, as a child." Odd, she thinks, that with all of her private terrors, she is the one who is fearless on the water.

Tom nods as if this makes perfect sense. "I took a couple out once, for their wedding anniversary," he says, "Her idea of a romantic time was to drift for two hours in the middle of the Bay, watch the sunset, then dock on Tilghman's Island for dinner and dancing. Well, I never saw a man less comfortable on a boat. He looked like he was going to throw his guts up the entire night." Tom gazes out over the water, where the afternoon sun sparkles on the tips of incoming waves. "He must have loved her a lot, that's all I can say."

So, Sarah wants to ask, *was Lily a water person?* And *How do you get used to being without her?* But she doesn't. Instead, she turns to look at the children, forces herself to think something motherly. Maddie and Zach are sitting slightly apart, each one turned a bit away from the other, as if they are afraid to get too close to a member of the opposite sex. Zach has a *Ranger Rick* magazine with him now and is explaining something to Maddie with the utmost earnestness. Probably a story about beetles who eat dung, Sarah thinks. Zach is delighted by anything having to do with excrement. Maddie crinkles her nose in distaste like a perfect little girl, then laughs in spite of herself, bending over the magazine to take a look.

There is a sweet, bold joy in Maddie, hiding behind the little girl's sadness. Sarah recognizes it in the exuberant pleasure Maddie takes in every flower, every leaf in Ginna's greenhouse. She had reacted with pure delight when Ginna walked her through the topiary garden and gave her a quick tour of the spacious greenhouse behind the house, suggesting that Maddie might like to help grow and sculpt a topiary creature for the garden. So far the two of them have attempted a unicorn (Maddie's idea) that became so lopsided it had to be shaved down to a small rabbit; and they are working on a family of hedgehogs that will be scattered in terra cotta pots across Ginna and Pat's back patio.

Maddie's drawing is also growing stronger. When the weather is nice, she and Zach spend Monday and Wednesday afternoons with Sarah and Ginna in the garden, sketching flowers and insects. Sarah has taught Maddie how to do quick, three minute sketches without lifting her pencil from the page, how to draw with her eyes closed, trusting her hand to capture the shape and gesture of a flower. Last week Maddie sketched a single yellow tulip, petals barely clasped shut, looking like it was bursting to open. "It's beautiful, sweetheart," Sarah breathed, watching the little girl's face light up and then cloud slightly, a change Maddie has learned to hide deftly by rubbing her nose vigorously with two fingers. "Let's save this one to show your dad, okay?"

Now she wants to explain this to Tom, the way Maddie's confidence shines on her face when she smiles, how she is smiling more often these days.

"My father's cancer is back," she says abruptly, her face turned away from Tom, tilted back so that she can feel the sun against her skin.

There. It wasn't so difficult, saying it. She doesn't even care whether Tom answers, is surprised to feel him cut off the engine and walk over to sit next to her. *He doesn't want to hear anything more about cancer,* she admonishes herself. *His wife just died of it, isn't that enough?*

Tom sighs next to her, a long, breathy sigh that seems to settle itself around her shoulders and bring her comfort.

"We should let the kids have lunch." Sarah announces. She unpacks the two bags of food, discovering that she is ravenously hungry. She lays out cheese sandwiches and peaches for the kids, gourmet ham and brie for herself and Tom, bags of Cheese Doodles and pita crisps and two small, beautiful cherry pies, their crusts decorated with sugary leaves of dough.

"I don't know what I was thinking," she says, not turning to face Tom. "That the doctors were all wrong? That he would be the one to escape, somehow?"

The wind whips hair across her face, stings her eyes. "It's like when you have a baby," she rushes on. "You look at him and you think, this is the most perfect thing, the best there will ever be. And for just a little while, you can actually believe that maybe your baby will be spared, that life won't crowd in and ruin him . . . But you know it will. And there's not one damned thing you can do but watch it happen."

She has forgotten to bring a knife, so she and Tom carve large wedges of pie from the tins with a plastic fork, setting them on napkins for Zach and Maddie to eat, licking gobs of cherry filling from their fingers. The pie is tart, and liquid and sweet, and maybe not as good as Ginna's banana crème, Sarah thinks, but certainly very close.

Sarah has heard friends describe the exact moment they knew that a marriage had run its course. Helene said she felt it in her hips, like a dead weight she had been carrying up a long, steep mountain. "It was time to let it go," she said simply. "Kind of like taking off a really heavy fanny pack." Does death come with signals like that, too? Sarah wants to ask about Lily's last day—was it a day like every other one before it except there weren't going to be any more?

Birth was so much more straightforward. You could chart the precise moment when labor pains started, when the cervix dilated, when the baby's head began to push through. Sarah's midwife had told her an ancient Chinese story: that when a child is about to be born, the Big Dipper tips in the night sky, spilling a shower of stars down toward the earth. The stars that land near the newborn infant form her path, the way she is meant to travel in life. When Daddy was born, Sarah wonders, did the stars that tumbled down near him point to this? Was there something that anyone could have foreseen?

"Don't you think," she asks, staring out over the water, "That there should be some clear sign when a life is about to end? So that we could prepare for it?" They are heading back towards Chesapeake Beach, and the end of their boat ride weighs on her uncomfortably.

She watches Tom's eyes soften. "There was a day when Lily and I knew—she knew before I did—that it wasn't going to be much longer. It was a hot morning, and she couldn't get comfortable in bed, the pain wouldn't quit. I kept bringing her cool washcloths for her forehead, turning up the ceiling fan. All the windows were thrown open to bring in a breeze. I was distracted, not really paying attention to her, and then I felt her staring at me, and everything slowed down. There was a look on her face, and I thought, No, no, today's not a good day at all, not today."

Tom stops, and Sarah sits absolutely still. "I wanted everything to be perfect—I thought she would be freshly washed and beautiful, not sweating like a pig, and that I would bring her favorite flavor of sherbet, lime. I thought we would have time to get ready, you know, to make it right. And then I realized, it's going to happen just like this—right in the thick of it—when the laundry isn't done and her hair smells bad and nothing is perfect at all. And I might not even be looking at her when it happens."

He is shaking his head. "I don't think you get many days like that."

"Like what?"

"I mean days when you can see things exactly as they are, crystal clear, not the way you want them to be. As if you're looking at your life through a magnifying glass, and you know that if the lens shifts even slightly, you'll lose it all."

After Row and Zach have fallen asleep that night, Sarah sits in her kitchen, sorting through photographs and sliding them into clear plastic sleeves. She is making an album for her father, one he can carry with him when he goes to the hospital. There will be more hospital stays, the doctors have warned them, perhaps very soon. She is trying to choose photos that will make him smile and remember, but she hates the way she looks in most of their family pictures. In some of them, her hair is too wild—she can hear her father saying, "It's time to cut that mop." Or the look on her face is too fixed, too frozen.

In every photograph Sarah has from her own childhood, her mother's face is drawn and tense, although she often smiles bravely into the camera lens. She looks, Sarah thinks, a lot like those photos of hostages, taken to convince their loved ones and the President of the United States that they're still alive. Sarah never wanted to be that kind of mother, but here she is, in photo after photo, with her mother's tired, tight smile.

She comes across her favorite photograph of Zach, one that her father had snapped in Central Park when Zach was only eighteen months old. It is a windy morning, and Zach's cheeks are red, his eyes glistening. Sarah and Row are tossing the baby up into the air between them, and he is laughing, big, delighted bursts of laughter. It is exactly as Tom described it, Sarah sees, the moment right before the lens shifts. The picture captures Zach up in the air, midway between Sarah and Row. He is poised between flying and falling, in that moment of pure, wild faith just before he will be caught up in a warm pair of arms and lofted toward the sky again.

Stan

It must be 85 degrees in the goddamned shade, Stan thinks as he swings ferociously at the ball. There is an awning stretched over part of the putting green that keeps out the sun, but the heat is already oppressive at eleven in the morning.

Stan shows Zach exactly where to stand, how to place his feet shoulder width apart, how to take a couple of practice swings before hitting the ball for good. Zach fidgets a little under his grandfather's touch, but he is watching Stan closely, trying hard to match every move, his small mouth twisted in concentration. He swings and misses, swings and misses again, and darts a look at Stan to see if he has disappointed his grandfather. Stan shakes his head and points to his knees, makes an exaggerated knee-bend motion. Delighted by the mimicking game, Zach bends his own knees, his little body bouncing back and forth. Stan is proud to see that Zach keeps his feet planted firmly on the ground while he swings. That's the most common mistake kids make when they're learning, he knows, dancing around too much with their feet.

"Aghinn!" Stan and Zach ignore the stares of the other golfers around them. Zach lines up another ball and tries again. When his club meets the ball with a satisfying thwack and sends it rolling a few feet across the green, the little boy is ecstatic. "I hit it, Grampa, I hit it, did you see?"

Stan nods energetically, a huge smile breaking over his own face.

"This kid is a natural!" he writes to Sarah at lunch. His daughter rolls her eyes and gets up to refill the iced tea pitcher. "Daddy always thought we were naturals at everything," she tells Lynda, without looking at Stan. "Abby was a natural at horseback riding; then he was convinced she was going to be a concert cellist; and I was going to be a famous artist…"

Well, you could have been, if you didn't always give up. Stan starts to write this and manages to stop himself, crossing out the sentence abruptly with his pen. It's one of the few advantages of not speaking out loud; by the time your brain has formed a thought and transmitted the signal to your hand, and your hand has clasped around a pen and begun to write, enough time elapses so that sometimes—just sometimes—you think better of what you were planning to say. He can feel Sarah's eyes on the notepad, however, and knows she guessed what he was thinking anyway. Zach jumps down from the table and tugs on Stan's arm. "Do you want to play outside, Grampa, do you?" This is the one who is going to be great, Stan tells himself as he heaves up from the kitchen table, ignoring the look that Lynda aims in his direction, and heads out into the back yard with Zach. Stan is not going to fail this child.

It is steaming hot—what was he thinking, visiting Maryland in

August?—and Stan can only play catch with Zach for about five tosses of the ball before he is having difficulty breathing. He finds a seat on a stone bench in the back yard and reaches for his handkerchief, coughing violently. The handkerchief is sprayed beet red with his blood in a matter of seconds. This is a new symptom, and one that Stan has no intention of sharing with his daughter. He had been opposed to telling Sarah and Abby about the latest MRI results, in fact, but Lynda—who Stan has taken to calling *Mein Fuhress* in his notes—insisted.

Zach is watching, wide-eyed, so Stan puts his notepad on his lap and forces his hand to write, stilling the tremors that are shaking his entire upper body with each cough. "Grandpa is OK," he scribbles, and then, "Don't tell Mommy. Our secret."

It's only because Stan wants to find a place to dispose of his handkerchief that they enter the house through the garage. Stan crumples the bloody cloth and tosses it into a trash bin and manages to steady his breathing. He pauses for a moment then to gather himself, and looks around. Sarah has transformed the garage into a studio space, with easels set up at child's height for Zach and huge sheets of butcher paper tacked up across the walls. On one wall the sheets of paper are crowded with painted prehistoric monsters that are clearly Zach's handiwork, and next to them are a set of more sophisticated paintings, some of flowers and others depicting beach scenes.

Zach runs to the wall where one of his paintings is hanging. "Look, Grampa, I made a picture of you!"

Stan steps closer. The little boy has outlined the shape of a huge winged monster in dark green, and added flowing orange flames that erupt from the creature's mouth. At the bottom of the page is a small stick figure with his arms thrown up to the sky. Long tendrils of fire travel from the dragon's mouth to wrap themselves around the throat of the little man. Stan feels his own throat constrict as he stares at the painting.

"That's your sickness, Grampa." Zach says matter-of-factly. "I can see it. That's what makes your insides burn."

Stan is not the kind of person to believe in redemption. But knowing that his grandson recognizes his suffering—has, in fact, assigned it a face and a color—is somehow an enormous relief. It brings him hope, if only for a moment, that when this ordeal is all over he might be forgiven.

He squeezes Zach's hand and points to his throat. The little boy reaches up a hand and touches his grandfather's neck. "It's the fire that makes you so angry all the time, right Grampa?"

Stan cannot find an answer. Turning away from the wall, he lands in front of a drafting table that holds two of Sarah's sketchpads. He opens one and flips through a series of pencil drawings, his hand shaking. Stan's astonishment deepens as he turns the pages. The sketches are exceptionally good. He can't tell what they are supposed to be, really—on most pages there are only tall, towering shapes. Some remind him of skyscrapers and others look like Buddhist temples. He stops at one page covered with long sweeping arcs that bring to mind the marvelous span of the Brooklyn Bridge, its 5900-foot leap across the East River. The powerful lines on the sketchbook pages convey the same ambition, the same hope that Stan believes must have stirred John Augustus Roebling, the German immigrant who dared to design the world's longest suspension bridge. There must be a sketchbook of Roebling's somewhere, like this one, that documents his first, early concept of what the bridge would look like.

Seeing Sarah's artwork steals Stan's last good breath. He feels the back of his throat closing and another coughing fit coming on. He is bent over, rasping and gargling, when Lynda opens the garage door. "Stan. What on earth are you doing out here? Come inside." He allows himself to be led back into the bright kitchen and fussed over, feeling slightly foolish and irritated that his glimpse of his daughter's drawings has been interrupted.

He looks at Sarah across the kitchen, her back to him as she reaches into the fridge to retrieve a juice box for Zach. Stan imagines her bristling at the thought of her father looking through the sketchbooks. Well, if she doesn't want him to know she has returned to her artwork, so be it. I can play that game, he thinks. Stan pats his leg and turns to pull Zach up onto his lap, ignoring his daughter. Mum's the word.

Sarah

Across the reception room at Sloan-Kettering Cancer Center, a mother waits for her son. The large room is carpeted in muted blues and greens, with low, comfortable sofas placed along the walls and under three tall windows. Classical music plays softly in the background. It's possible to believe, for a moment, that the people waiting here are not ravaged by something with a power far beyond art or reason. They wait a long time, shifting on square plastic seats in front of the receptionist's desk, Lynda talking to her office on a cell phone and Sarah and Abby sitting in silence on either side of their father. The mother across the room waits, too, for her teenage son to come out of the doctor's office. When he finally emerges and crosses the room she rises with a sad smile, her whole body stretching towards him, and smooths his hair back from his face, a tiny hesitant gesture. She asks him something—which arm they put the IV in this time?—and when the boy points to his left arm his mother bends over heavily and gives him a kiss, one single, deliberate kiss in the bandaged crook of his elbow, then turns away as if she cannot bear to look at him one second longer. Sarah wants to go to her and say, *I know. Look, I know.*

She is in New York for her father's first chemo appointment.

After many weeks of waiting—for biopsy results, for consultations with the radiation expert, the pain management specialist and the oncologist—her father's mouth began to bleed, a sign that the tumors in his mouth would not wait. He could no longer eat solid foods, and was living on mashed potatoes, soup, and vanilla Peptamen. The last time Sarah called, he could barely speak.

There is no new way to see this, Sarah thinks, to hold it up to the light and reveal a truth that no one has uncovered before. It did not surprise her when the oncologist told them that chemotherapy would, at best, buy her father six months. She has been waiting for this, for precisely these words to be spoken. She and Abby and Lynda had listened gravely and nodded, thanked the doctor and left his office quickly.

Feeling loss before it happens has always been Sarah's strong point. She used to cry at night in her bed, imagining her cat dying or the family doctor taking her aside to explain gently that her mother had a terminal illness. Testing to see how that would feel—like probing a loose tooth to discover the exact shape of the hole it will leave behind—and how she would stand up to it. Being able to stand up to things, that was the challenge.

Sometimes, now, she thinks she can begin to see what living without her father will be like. She feels it in her neck and shoulders at odd moments, the sharp tang of his absence, the way her body anticipates a fever before it comes on, and she begins to assemble what she will need to get through it: orange juice, extra-strength Tylenol, Sleepytime tea with honey. She has no idea what she will need to get through this. It is like packing for a journey to a distant land, where she will not be quite herself, where the inhabitants speak a different language. Where you can be taught to politely say "Good afternoon" and "Where is the bathroom, please?" but after that your powers of translation simply run out. You will never again be able to say exactly what you mean and trust that anyone will understand you.

"Mr. Gershman?" the nurse calls out. It is their father's turn now, to get his blood drawn and then to sit behind a curtain while an IV tube drains colorless liquid into his veins. He lies down on the hospital bed with a grunt, clicks the television to ESPN, and closes his eyes. Sarah, Abby and Lynda take turns sitting with him, eyeing the TV or watching the slow drip of the drug.

Some of the people behind the other curtains in this large, open room are playing cards or checkers with their wives and husbands during chemo, talking quietly, or reading books. They wear the battle-weary looks of those who have been here before, who have incorporated this Monday afternoon visit into the rhythm of their week. Sarah is unnerved by the respectful quiet. She would be more comfortable if someone were weeping, if somebody's sister or daughter stood up directly in front of the nurses' station flapping her arms up and down and yelling, NO.

She watches her father sleep the way she watched Zach when he was an infant, checking to make sure he was still breathing, feeling a constant connection to the life that pulsed through his body. She imagined the blood swelling tiny vessels on its way to his heart and brain. Now, watching her father's chest rise and fall with his breath, she pictures the cancer blossoming and trying to take hold, the radiation scorching away layer upon layer of tumor, chemo pitting his cells against each other in a primal battle. She is unable to banish the military metaphors from her mind, and none of them are comforting.

They wait and watch for an hour, until the last drop from the IV has penetrated her father's bloodstream. He has fallen asleep, and the nurse shakes him gently awake. It is time to go home. Sarah says goodbye and catches a cab to the train station, wishing, as she hugs her father outside the hospital, that he would not let go, that he would hang on to her for dear life, that he would stop traffic on 67nd Street to hold his daughter for a very, very long time.

She boards the Metroliner, stands in line at the café car to buy a bottle of spring water, hands the conductor her ticket, stares out the window at the darkening sky. Sarah's cell phone rings a couple of hours later, just as she is ready to doze off. Her body has finally relaxed against the seat; she has given herself over to the train's easy, gentle beat. Scrambling to locate her purse on the seat next to her, she struggles to focus, finds the phone, irritated. It's Rowland, calling to check in with her.

"So where are you?" he asks, and then swiftly adds, "No, don't tell me. You're crossing the Chesapeake on the northern end, heading into Baltimore."

There is silence on Sarah's end of the line. She can tell Row is trying not to get impatient. "Remember?" he coaxes, "Remember when the train crossed over a big expanse of water?"

Sarah thinks back, her mind blank. She has been staring out the window ever since the train rolled out of Penn Station, but without consciously registering the landscape, only feeling it tug at her every once in a while. The last thing she remembers noticing was the bridge out of Trenton, with its bold, illuminated letters proclaiming, "Trenton Makes. The World Takes."

Just after they hang up, and Sarah has nestled herself into the seat again, her jacket thrown over her legs as a blanket, the train crosses a long, low bridge over the Chesapeake Bay, the water gleaming and choppy below. Sarah feels comforted that Rowland was right. Her husband has found her. He knows exactly where she is on the map and where she will be five minutes from now and five minutes after that, until the moment she arrives at home. It's a handle on the movements of the people he loves that Sarah envies.

She remembers when Zach was little enough that she could still track all of his movements, know every step he took around their house or out back in the garden. How odd it was, after six months, to leave him in the morning for work, unlatching herself from those daily rhythms. It left her feeling loose, without moorings. For the first two months, she demanded that the babysitter write down every hour of the day, and next to the time, what Zach was doing, so that Sarah could recapture, by reading the notes, exactly how her son had spent his time. She saved some of those daily logs, and still looks at them from time to time. "10 a.m.," they said, "fed and changed diaper. Baby fell asleep. 12:00 p.m., one hour outside playing on his blanket. Very hot. Ate mashed squash."

She thinks of how much Row hates to navigate in new terrain. Even shopping in a new grocery store can make him uncharacteristically grouchy. He needs to know precisely where the eggs and the milk will be when he enters a store, where to find his favorite brand of soap or deodorant. Of course he was able to plot the exact location of her train. It's what he is good at.

"New Carrollton station next, followed by D.C. Union Station. New Carrollton in about 25 minutes, followed by D.C." The Amtrak agent in his trim blue cap and uniform plucks Sarah's seat check from above her head and continues down the aisle, the faces of passengers turning up briefly as he passes. *Another person who knows precisely where we are*, Sarah thinks, and she lets herself be soothed by the man's low, even voice, his pleasant smile, the rock back and forth of the train cars as they roll toward Washington. She breathes in deeply and smells aftershave—or maybe men's cologne?—and wonders idly who is wearing it. It smells good, deep and pungent, like lemons and ginger. Row used to wear something like this, and Sarah would burrow her mouth and nose into the soft curve where his neck meets his shoulder, where sweat gathers in warm weather, where a man's scent always seems to be the thickest. *When was the last time I did that*, she wonders. *We don't smell each other any more*, she wants to say to her husband. She will tell him that tonight, Sarah thinks sleepily, and he will look at her as if she has gone crazy.

Stan

For a sweet while, chemo does not make him sick. In fact, the drug lulls him to sleep like a baby, stops the spinning in his brain. The steady plink, plink of the IV bag, the nurse's cool hand on his arm, adjusting the blood pressure cuff, ESPN droning in the background. He falls into a dreamless sleep every time, the hours of waiting and worrying swirling away down to nothing. When the nurse wakes him up, he feels refreshed. Really, how crazy is that? Chemo, the new path to inner peace.

Stan entered chemotherapy the way other men before him had volunteered for military service, signing on to a fight he could only dimly imagine. Praying he was up to the challenge. This fight was his and yet not his, a struggle of his body against parts of itself. Mingled with his rage and horror at what his body has become is a fear of dishonor so deep it propels him to this hospital bed twice a week, where he sleeps and waits to feel stronger. Waits for a sign that he is going to make it, that he deserves to survive.

And one day, when the bag finishes dripping and Stan opens his eyes, Millie is there. She is simply there: an apparition from his past, sitting on the green plastic chair next to his bed with a paperback novel open in her lap. Since that day she has appeared regularly on Mondays, the one day when Lynda doesn't accompany Stan to his regular chemo appointment. He has never asked Millie how she knows.

When Stan opens his eyes and sees her for the first time he tears up, he can't help it. Without missing a beat, Millie reaches into her purse and hands him a Kleenex. It smells like her lilac hand lotion, and the fragrance—from over twenty years ago—hits him like a slap. "Still a big softie," Millie says. Her face is sad but there is a smile behind her eyes. "We're getting older but not tougher, huh, Stan?"

Stan wants to answer but can't. He nods his head emphatically, clearing his throat with a helpless gargling sound and flashing her his biggest smile.

At first he doesn't want her there, at the hospital. Millie was with him in his glory days, she knows him like nobody else does. She was the office secretary when he worked for Senator Jacob Javits. He thinks he doesn't want anyone from the old days to see him like this. But then he realizes, Who am I kidding? Before he knows what's happening, he is looking forward to his Monday morning appointments.

They reminisce about their days working together, the long nights spent typing and revising draft after draft of the legislation that would become the nation's first workers' compensation law. Those were heady days, when Stan first recognized that he was part of something far-reaching, something more substantial than himself.

Millie isn't there when he arrives one Monday morning, so Stan flips idly through the magazines in the waiting room: old, worn issues of *Sports Illustrated* and *National Geographic*. He picks up last month's *National Geographic* and begins reading an article about pandas while he waits to be called.

He learns something new every time he reads *National Geographic*. Bamboo, it turns out, is the one food pandas depend upon, but they have to eat massive quantities of the stuff in order to get the nutrients they need. *Adult pandas typically spend 12 hours each day eating bamboo, and they can consume more than 80 lbs of the plant's leaves and stalks.*

Nature is completely illogical, Stan thinks. Why create an animal that has to eat all day just to stay alive? More to the point, why stick it in a remote mountain forest in China where bamboo is the only food source around, if bamboo doesn't provide the nutrition to sustain the species?

He puts down the magazine, feeling mildly betrayed. He reads *National Geographic* to be reassured that the natural order of things is still in place, that in the physical world at least, everything is behaving as it should. It is soothing to learn about the grooming behavior of gorillas, or to discover that scientists are hard at work trying to solve the mystery of why sea turtles in New Zealand mate for life.

Today's article about pandas strikes him as not only illogical but alarming. As if the force of nature, which he assumes holds us all tightly within its intricate, multi-layered web, had suddenly snapped a few threads. He reads on, and it only gets worse:

Even such huge quantities of bamboo, however, cannot provide the proteins and fatty acids required to nourish more than one baby panda. The female panda produces barely enough milk to nurse one cub after birth. If she has two cubs, she must make a cruel choice, choosing one to abandon.

Stan thinks about the pandas while he waits for Millie, while the drugs enter his dumb animal arm and stream through his veins. Thinks about the absence of logic in the natural world. About a mother panda, deciding between two cubs.

Stan is nine, and his brother Robbie is eleven. There is no doubt in his mind that if his mother were forced to choose which of her two sons should die, she would let Stan go. His mother loves him, he knows that; he can feel the sturdiness of her love in the way she tugs his jacket on in the mornings before school and kisses him on the cheek, saying, "Off to school, my little man." But her love for Robbie runs deeper, is more helpless, akin to the swoon a woman feels in the presence of her lover. Robbie has their mother under a spell. He is the high achiever, Stan always the ordinary one. Stan is small for his age, and has never been good at sports, unless you count table tennis. Robbie is good at everything—football, golf, school—and he is their mother's favorite. He can tell by the way their mother looks at her two sons that she would leave Stan alone in the wilderness if it meant she could keep her firstborn, her baby, alive.

Robbie has a doctor's appointment today, and Stan is sure that the doctor is a little in love with his mother. Men fall in love with her everywhere she goes—waiters, busboys, the clerk at the delicatessen down the street. Why should this doctor be any different? When Mother leans in close with her perfumed hair and those big green eyes and wide lipsticked mouth and says, "Doctor, don't you dare tell me my little boy is not going to have another birthday!" how could the doctor help himself?

His father was the one to tell him that Robbie was very sick. His mother hardly said a word to Stan during the entire final month when his brother lay in a hospital bed, his small body looking smaller every day. She kissed Stan absently goodnight before he went upstairs, and she asked him "How was school today?" if she happened to be home when he got off the bus.

The one time Stan dared to ask when Robbie was going to come home, his mother dropped the coffee cup she was holding and left the dining room without a word. His father, a man who could not stand to see his wife unhappy, slammed one hand flat on the table, making the forks and spoons jump. "Can't you see you're upsetting your mother?" He rarely raised his voice to his sons, and in this instance he didn't need to—Stan was already miserably aware that he had done the wrong thing. He never asked his mother about Robbie again, and she never offered any additional information.

He learned to make salami sandwiches. Spectacular sandwiches, heaps of sliced salami dripping with brown mustard, that he made for himself after school. He ate standing up alone at the kitchen counter, washing down the sandwich with milk straight from the bottle. When he thinks of that month, it's the one vivid memory that comes flooding back: the taste of salami with mustard on rye, the kind his father always ordered at the deli.

When Robbie died, Uncle Lou took him aside, slipped ten dollars into his hand and told him to be strong for his mother's sake.

Stan needed no further instructions. He glanced around the living room where the family was sitting *shiva*, studying the scene carefully: the women clustered around his mother in an intimate, swarming circle like a hive of bees, the men sitting silently, balancing paper plates of whitefish and taking big bites out of their bagels. Each man was his own solitary, private universe, Stan saw—his creased pants leg spread apart, inscribing the boundaries around him. Stan would command his own universe one day, and he understood. It was time to begin preparations. He tucked away his deep sorrow about Robbie, like something that could be folded and contained within one of the pocket handkerchiefs his mother had given him for his birthday last year, cream with his initials, "SG" stitched in navy blue thread.

"Mr. Gershman."

Stan rubs his eyes, jamming the heels of his hands into his eye sockets. The nurse is shaking him awake, and there is another voice, too.

"Stan." Millie.

He opens his eyes groggily, takes in Millie's tentative smile, her hand on his shoulder. He reaches for her hand, thinks how soft it is, like his mother's. Still in the grip of sleep, of his dream, he has a moment of utter clarity. He needs to tell her, to explain: this is why the cancer makes no sense, why it has him feeling that the universe has been turned on its head. He sees it now. Stan isn't the one who was supposed to succumb to illness—that was Robbie. Stan was meant to survive, and to be hated for it.

Sarah

The monarch butterflies have left their homes early this year, as if they know that something is not right, as if their timing has been thrown off. They gather in the air this September morning in brilliant swarms of orange and black, and if Sarah tips her head back she sees an entire quivering world of them, dipping up and down in waves, lush and bright against the steely gray of the sky. Each year in early fall the monarchs fly through yards and above patios in suburban Cape May, New Jersey, grandly announcing their departure for the warmer air in the mountains of Mexico, where they will spend the winter. In an astounding feat of nature, millions of butterflies make their way across the continent, flying forty or fifty miles a day, faithfully returning to the same hilltops that have sheltered monarchs for hundreds of years. Somehow they manage to find their way to a place they have never visited, often landing on the exact fir trees where their ancestors wintered decades earlier.

Zach has never seen the migration, and he stands with Sarah outside the beach house watching in stunned silence, reaching one small hand up into the air—to stop the flood of wings? to witness by touch how they feel? How one butterfly and one more and one more and another become, together, something elemental, thousands of wings pulsing as a single organism, driven into movement across a morning sky.

Sarah and Row rented the house on Cape May Point for Labor Day weekend, and it is beginning to seem like the longest three days of Sarah's life. Two months ago, a vacation at the beach with her father seemed like just the thing. A perfect rest for him after finishing a round of chemo, a time to be surrounded by family. Abby couldn't make the trip east from Seattle at this time of year, so it was just the five of them: Daddy, Lynda, Sarah, Row and Zach.

It is his eyes that bother her the most, Sarah decides. The skin around her father's eyes has bent into damp, uneven folds, giving him the presence of a much softer man. This man whose rage could shake the walls of their suburban ranch house when she and Abby were little, whose arguments with their mother were legendary in the family, is smaller now, reduced. He does not want her to know him this way. And so he will no longer look her squarely in the eyes. When Sarah speaks he glances up slowly, focusing on a space just to the right of her head, the way very elderly people do, taking her in with his peripheral vision perhaps, but refusing to meet his daughter's gaze. His eyes remind her of the round black eyes on Zach's favorite stuffed dinosaur, pinkish and unraveling around the edges.

Late last night, long after Row had taken Zach upstairs to bed,

Sarah, Lynda and her father sat together in the small screened-in porch. Her father began talking about where he wanted to be buried, discussing death as if it was something that will happen to him. "Plot at B'nai Abraham in Brooklyn," he scribbled on a yellow notepad.

"Is that where Grandpa is?" Sarah asked.

Her father nodded vigorously and wrote some more. "And my grandparents." He and Lynda exchanged a look, and Sarah's stomach clenched. "What?"

It turned out that her father wants Lynda to be buried next to him when she dies. But B'nai Abraham is an Orthodox Jewish cemetery, and Lynda isn't Jewish, so in order to be buried there, she would need to convert to Judaism.

"Do you want to convert?" Sarah had asked. "It's a really big deal, a long process. It's not something you can just decide overnight."

She couldn't believe they hadn't considered this before. Each day she feels her father's funeral pressing down on all of them, an event they needed to think through, to be prepared for. Why weren't they prepared?

Lynda looked away for a long time before answering. "I've always thought I would be cremated," she said finally.

"You've always thought?" Sarah blurted out. "Well, did Daddy know that?" She can tell from her father's face, drawn and sad, that he is hearing this for the first time. Sarah hates Lynda at that moment, wants to shout at her for even contemplating letting her father be buried alone. She can picture Lynda's ashes sprinkled carefully, neatly somewhere over the reservoir in Central Park, while Daddy lies in Brooklyn, surrounded by generations of agitated Gershmans and Horowitzes, all prodding him, wondering, "*Nu?* Where's your wife?"

"Don't you two ever talk to each other?" Sarah had wished desperately that she could shut up, had wanted Abby there with her. Abby would have touched her shoulder, given her a warning glance, telegraphing: Cool it. Enough. But Sarah found herself unable to stop talking. "When were you going to plan this stuff?" she demanded. Her father and Lynda looked at each other in silence.

Sarah had finally pushed her chair back in disgust and gone upstairs to her bedroom, taking her wine glass and the half-empty bottle of Cabernet from the dinner table. Row and Zach were already sound asleep, struck by too much sun. Sarah had meant to call Abby, to share this latest drama with her sister, but instead she drank the wine, slowly and purposefully, until the bottle was empty, and fell asleep on top of the covers.

Today, Sarah and Lynda are pretending that last night's conversation never happened. Zach is refusing to go to the beach. "I don't have a good time there," he wails. "I hate the beach." Sarah remembers that last year, he had been bothered by the grit of sand between his toes and inside his swim trunks, but once he was in the ocean, he had a glorious time splashing in the waves. He refuses to remember the joy of the water, and she cannot persuade him to try it. She sits at the rickety kitchen table by the window sipping coffee, wishing she had a son who could see the positive side of things, wishing she had been born into any family but this one.

"Grampa, um, do you want to play Legos?" Zach stands hesitantly in the doorway of the small den where his grandfather sits watching television. At any other time, Zach's voice would be enough to bring a huge smile to his grandfather's face. Today, however, he gets no response. "Daddy," Sarah calls out loudly, "Zach wants to play, do you feel up to it?" Her father waves his hand dismissively in their direction without turning his head.

"Sweet pie, Grandpa's very tired right now, maybe you can play with him later." Sarah reaches out for Zach, but he bolts and runs over to his grandfather, begins climbing onto his lap.

Rowland comes into the kitchen just then in his favorite pair of worn khaki shorts, ready for a late morning run. "Aren't you guys coming to the beach?" he asks, reaching out a hand lazily to stroke Sarah's hair. He looks suntanned and vaguely content, and in that moment Sarah can recognize nothing about Row that is familiar, nothing that she can grab hold of to save her. She admires her husband from afar, her eyes scanning the spray of dark hair on his bare chest the way she would view a particularly lovely sculpture in an art museum. She sends him off to the beach with a smile, reminding him to take sunblock and to look for the butterflies. It is only after the front door clicks shut behind him that she realizes she has been holding her breath, waiting for her husband to leave.

She hears a loud thud from the next room, and a split second later, Zach is wailing. "Dad! What happened?" Her father has one hand pressed to his eyes and refuses to meet her gaze. Sarah stands in front of him for a moment, then scoops up her sobbing son and heads upstairs.

In Mexico, there is a legend that says that the monarch butterflies returning to the mountains each year carry the spirits of our ancestors, bringing them home to visit. *What part of us is our spirit?* Sarah wonders. She imagines it as the distilled essence of a person, both good and bad, all of our possibilities and our failures. She tries hard to imagine that this is true, that each of the things that make up her father's unique character—his crazy moves on the dance floor, the way he loved to read "Green Eggs and Ham" aloud to his daughters in a heavy British accent, his infectious laugh or his passion for the Yankees—could endure, could travel lightly on butterfly wings on the cool fall winds, two thousand miles to Mexico City.

She is finding it harder and harder to believe that anything persists after a person dies. Watching her father, in fact, she feels that he is disappearing already, receding into himself.

She walks over to where her father is sitting in front of the television. She has settled Zach upstairs with his stuffed dinosaurs and a puzzle. Piles of books and magazines surround her father's armchair, heaped on the footstool and the floor, and Sarah begins, automatically, to pick them up, straightening the piles. Her father has fallen asleep, his mouth slack, arms crossed loosely over an old Seattle Philharmonic T-shirt, his hands fallen open. He naps several times a day now, sometimes all morning. This is his life: waking and sleeping, sleeping and waking, pain and the absence of pain. On the television, Roger Moore is making witty conversation with a voluptuous woman in an old James Bond movie. Sarah has never much liked Roger Moore; Sean Connery was, in her opinion, a much better Agent 007. Roger Moore seems too aloof for the role. Sean Connery has more warmth, more passion to get the bad guys. He reminds Sarah, in fact, of her father.

Sarah has lived her entire life knowing that her father was someone whose work was vital, a prominent attorney with connections in Congress and on Wall Street, someone who had lunch with senators and real estate moguls. She and Abby accepted their father's importance as a given, attending award ceremonies and watching him on television, marching confidently down the courthouse steps after a particularly important case. Seeing him work late into the night, sometimes every night, and knowing without question that it was worth it. And yet Sarah sees now that her father does not believe this, does not think it has all added up to anything, sees it in the droop of his shoulders, the way his eyes slide closed, the exhaustion that catches him unawares several times a day.

She stands beside his chair and fights the urge to wake him, to press her lips to his ear and whisper, *please. Don't give up.* Her hands pause, and hover, then clasp themselves tightly together as she watches her father sleep, feeling how feeble her love is against the stupendous advancing strength of his illness. She turns off the light and leaves him, walks silently into the kitchen to make tuna sandwiches for lunch.

On the phone with Abby that evening, Sarah tries to make her sister understand. "He's worse now, Abby, he's—I don't know, fading away. And I keep thinking he's supposed to tell us things before he dies, not just clam up and leave."

"Jesus, Sarah, haven't you had enough?" Abby asks quietly. "I mean, isn't it time someone else got a word in? The man hasn't stopped talking his entire life."

It is true. Their father could develop an instant opinion about almost any subject, from buying the perfect outdoor grill to why women would never achieve complete equality in the workplace. He was prepared to defend his opinions, vigorously, against anyone who challenged him. Sarah has never managed to make a major life decision without consulting her father. She had even asked him what he thought of Row, when they began dating seriously. Her father liked Row, had taken him aside on their wedding day to say, "Whatever you're doing to make my daughter stop taking herself so seriously and start having some fun, you keep doing it."

"Sar, through all the bullshit, he loves you and wants you to be happy." Abby's voice cuts in. "You know that, right?"

"I hate it when you give me that big sister voice," Sarah answers grumpily.

"Yeah, okay. I love you, too."

Sarah hangs up feeling foolish, and sits on her bed with the telephone receiver still gripped in one hand. Just like Zach, she realizes. He is old enough to answer the phone by himself now, but he hasn't learned yet how to hang up when a conversation has run its course. He will hang on and on, driving Sarah and Row crazy, listening to the hum on the line, savoring the solid, grown-up feeling of the receiver in his small hand, the thrill of possession, the magic of holding on to a connection. *This is my problem*, Sarah thinks: *not knowing when I'm supposed to let go.* She lies in bed listening to the trees rustle outside, thinking of leaves falling, of things shedding and letting go, of casting her fears, her hopes and dreams out on the water and watching them bob away. She slows her breathing down, hoping for sleep.

Stan

Something animal rears up inside Stan when his grandson clambers onto his lap. Zach's foot kicks the shin of his aching leg, where he had the vascular surgery two years ago, still hurts like crazy on some days, and in that instant Stan can not summon one drop of love for this child. All that resounds in his brain is the need to get the kid off me, for Chrissake, get him away. With a great shove, he gets the kid off his lap. Hears the thump on the floor with just a tiny bit of satisfaction, if he must be honest. Reptilian brain, isn't that what the neuroscientists call it? When we are reduced to our animal selves, driven by small clumps of cells in the brain stem that control basic instincts—feeding, fighting, fleeing, and sex.

Sex, ha. Lynda has not turned towards him in bed for months, and most nights Stan is too exhausted to care. His body is fast becoming something alien to him, the primal animal parts overwhelming everything else that he knows. He is all reptile today, cold and scaly. His leg aches and his entire neck throbs and he hasn't gone to the bathroom in four days. A fact that he has managed to hide from his wife, who otherwise would fuss about calling the doctor. Christ, who wants a wife who tracks your bowel movements?

"Dad!" He closes his eyes against the irritating sound of his daughter's voice. She has come into the room to pick up Zach, who is sobbing. Stan's reptile eyes remain closed. He imagines them as puffy slits in a cold leathery face. "Sorry, sweetie, I'm tired," he tries to say, managing only a guttural mumble. He lifts a hand in their direction and hopes they will both go away. He only opens his eyes once Sarah stomps upstairs with Zach in her arms and the room is silent again. Beams of late morning sun slant through the window and if he shifts in just the right way in his armchair, the sun will begin to warm his legs under the blanket. He thinks fleetingly about his grandson, knows he will need to make peace later, but not right now. Right now he needs a nap.

He needs a nap but he does not sleep. He scrunches his eyes shut, thinking of nothing, trying to see past the insides of his own eyelids to the peace beyond, the blackness of rest. Picturing nothing makes Stan's eyes fly open again, and he stares straight ahead at the doorway. Thinking he is probably going straight to hell for making Zach cry. He reaches for his pain pills, fumbles one, two, orange tablets into his mouth, trying to remember when he took the last one but failing. He lifts his water glass, swishes water far back into his throat, and, tipping his head until his neck muscles clench, swallows.

He does not believe in hell, not really, doesn't think there is an afterlife. It wouldn't be accurate to say his faith is shaken by this illness—it was never very solid to begin with. In truth, God always seemed weightless, vague, not like anything that Stan could get his arms around. He remembers Sarah and Abby asking about God as little girls. Evie was always the one who answered their questions, who made up simple stories about a Creator, a benevolent force in the universe, about the need to do good and to make the world a better place. Stan believes in *tikkun olam*, in trying to heal the world, has certainly struggled to make a meaningful contribution with his work. But he falters trying to understand the purpose behind it all. It just stands to reason that there must be something beyond human existence, something more than our reptile brains following the path laid by a chain of DNA hundreds of thousands of years ago.

Sarah was a thinker and a doubter, just like him. Both girls went to Hebrew school on Sundays, and attended temple on the important holidays: Rosh Hashanah and Yom Kippur. But Sarah was the one who took it seriously. She joined the temple youth group and came home singing Hebrew folk songs and talking about visiting Israel. For a year in high school, she insisted that they light Shabbat candles every Friday night; then her interest in boys took over and she didn't seem to notice when Evie no longer brought the candles out. Sarah was his seeker, the daughter who could never be happy, who was always searching for a new answer.

He has a sudden memory of Sarah on the roof. As a teenager, she had discovered that she could slip out an upstairs window of her bedroom onto the gently sloping roof of the family room three feet below. She would lie flat on her back out there, her body pressed against the warm asphalt tile of the roof, eyes wide open, taking in the entire blue sky. All of it, from the broccoli tips of the trees in the backyard to the wispy grey of the clouds far away over the marsh.

"Stan!" His wife had shrieked when she discovered Sarah's hiding place, caught Sarah out on the roof one day. "She'll kill herself! It's dangerous out there! You tell her right this minute she can't go out there anymore!"

"Oh, Evie," Stan had said mildly, with a quick sideways wink at Sarah. "She'll be careful, I'm sure." He thought he understood why his daughter was out on the roof. He understood the ache to see it all, to be encircled by the broad expanse of sky, to throw your arms and legs wide apart and lie there soaking in the boundless, shimmering world. A longing so huge it hurt the inside walls of your chest when you breathed.

I don't know, he wants to say to Sarah. I don't know if we can ever make anything better. I don't know if it's possible to hold all of this wanting in our hearts and not break apart.

Sarah

Sarah has developed a sixth sense for late night phone calls. Since they returned home from Cape May, she has been having trouble sleeping, and she finds herself rolling over in bed some nights to reach for the phone seconds before it actually rings. Tonight it is Tom, his voice laced with a terror that makes Sarah sit straight up in bed, blinking hard to wake up. Maddie is gone. He has searched everywhere, in the house and the barn. The last time he saw his daughter was at bedtime, eight o'clock, when he tucked her into bed and went out to work on the boat. Sarah searches groggily for her clock on the nightstand. It is nearly one-thirty in the morning.

"Can you come?" he asks. It is the voice of a man who has seen how quickly love can slip away, how suddenly solid ground crumbles beneath the sturdiest of feet.

"Ten minutes." Sarah promises. She slides out of bed and scrawls a note to Row on the dining room table, quieting Connie with a pat as she grabs her keys and purse. She drives the eight miles to Tom's farm too quickly, squinting to see on the dark country roads, her heart jumping as if it were her own child lost out there in the night somewhere. *Stop it*, she tells herself impatiently, *this is ridiculous*.

When she reaches the house Tom is pacing in the driveway

with two flashlights, his face furrowed with shadows from the dim light on the porch. His arms hang, stunned, at his sides. Without thinking, Sarah reaches out to him and they hug. Only then is Sarah suddenly conscious of his breath on the back of her neck, her breasts pressing against the flannel of his shirt, nipples tightening in the night air. God, she hadn't even bothered to put on a bra. "Let me go down to the barn," she says, breaking away hurriedly. "There are a few places I can think of to look. You stay close to the house in case—I mean, so you're here when she comes back."

She begins walking in the direction of the old tobacco barn until she is sure that Tom can no longer see her, then she turns and heads toward the dock, calling Maddie's name. This is the one place Maddie is forbidden to go, and it is the place where Sarah is guessing the little girl will be. The edge of land, where water begins and things seem possible. The night is full of sound, the throaty calls of frogs from the marsh and the steady droning of insects in the poplar trees, branches scraping, somewhere in the distance a dog's warning bark.

A tree limb snaps and Sarah feels it in her stomach like a punch. She will not allow herself to picture Maddie drowned or lost, her sense of direction pulled out from under her. Alone in the warm, dark night buzzing with noise, unsure which path will take her back towards anything she can recognize as home. Sarah concentrates fiercely on the soft, low beam of her flashlight on the ground ahead, its pale circle meeting the black silhouettes of Boston fern and wild rhododendron.

She can smell the creek long before she reaches it, a salty, pungent scent heavy in the humid night air. She finds Maddie out by the water, huddled in a miserable lump at the end of the swaying dock.

The water is choppy, slapping harshly against the wooden planks, and
Sarah has to put out her arms to steady herself as she walks. Maddie
stands before Sarah has even reached her, as if she has been waiting to
be found, and slips her small, cold hands into Sarah's. "I can't feel her
anywhere," the little girl says after a moment, in a flat, exhausted voice.

"Your mother?" Sarah asks.

Maddie nods, her face crumpling. "She said I would always be
able to feel her with me out here."

Sarah remembers then Tom describing how Lily would play
long games of hide and seek with her daughter, the two of them
challenging each other like sisters or best friends, devising more and
more inventive hiding places each time they played—in the drying loft
of the tobacco barn, behind the rusting harvester, down among the
cattails that gathered in tall clumps along the pond. Maddie might have
been out here for hours, searching. She holds the girl tightly against
her, letting Maddie wail. The little girl cries in heaving sobs, the kind
she couldn't cry at her mother's funeral.

An hour later Sarah is sitting in the big farmhouse kitchen
alone with Tom, sipping hot chocolate laced with cognac. Maddie had
fallen into an exhausted sleep almost as soon as Tom lowered her into
bed, covering his daughter's face with kisses. He held her until she was
deeply asleep, her breathing slow and even, delicate white hands
unfurling against the blankets. He might have stayed in the darkened
room all night, watching Maddie sleep, if Sarah hadn't touched his
shoulder and suggested a hot drink.

"I tell her that her mom is always with her, watching over her,"
Tom says after they have settled into their chairs, staring into his mug of

cocoa. "But it's a pretty empty thing to say to an eight-year-old, you know?"

Sarah agrees. "It's as stupid as people telling you, Oh, she had such a good life." They drink cocoa silently for a while. Sarah stares at the scuffed surface of the table, glances down at her hands, anything to avoid the sadness that is alive in the air between them.

She is not astonished when he kisses her. One minute her eyes are glued to the table, the next instant Tom's mouth is on her hair. Perhaps he had expected her to pull away; but Sarah's lips recognize the potent swell of desperation and bruised hope in his kiss. His grief, still so fresh, makes them both reckless. They do not bother to go down the hall into Tom's bedroom. He undresses her on the broad wooden table in the kitchen, sliding down her blue jeans and reaching for the warm backs of her thighs. Sarah has lost herself so completely that she does not even think of Maddie in the next room, and barely feels Tom covering her mouth with his sweatshirt, burying her face in the salty smell that lingers on his clothes.

Afterward, lying on his bed, Sarah feels awake and strangely calm. Unleashed from her daily routine, no hurry at all to move. She wonders fleetingly if she could be one of those women who leaves a note on the fridge for their husbands—*Meatloaf defrosting. Towels in the dryer. Cat needs to be fed*—and walks out the door. No. But if she stays here, she will start to think about staying longer.

"I have to go," she says, trying not to let it sound like a rebuke. Tremors are still running down her thighs. She draws her clothes on hurriedly, rinses her cocoa mug in the big porcelain sink and lays it gently on the drainboard. Tom stands behind her, wrapping his arms around her shoulders.

"I don't know what to say," he begins, but Sarah will not let him finish. She turns and rocks him for a little while the way she had rocked Maddie, feeling him hold back his despair, tuck it away neatly somewhere where it will not spill out again anytime soon.

Someday she will tell Maddie about the monarch butterflies, she thinks, driving slowly away from the warm light of Tom's kitchen, trying to swallow the wild careening of her heart. She will explain to Maddie that the butterflies carry our ancestors' spirits lightly toward home. That it is possible for the ones we love to depart and yet to return, again and again, to hide in the places they love the best.

It doesn't surprise Sarah, entirely, that she lets herself see Tom more than just that once. She longs for him with an intensity she knows she should not trust, hungry for his abandon and his unpredictability. She enjoys his lopsided smile, loves that he doesn't even strive for perfection, his carelessness such a stark opposite to her husband's precise scripts for each day: gray silk tie, lunch with the head of the department, salad with blue cheese dressing on the side, no croutons and no carrots, please.

Row's decisiveness, his very particular tastes, used to make Sarah feel protected. Here was a man who knew what he wanted and would always be able to get it, who would be able to find her what she needed, too. Lately, however, everything about her husband infuriates her. At a time when randomness seems to be the new order of things, when her life has been split, yawning, open, Rowland's keen sense of order seems sadly misplaced.

When Tom kisses her Sarah feels devoured whole, taken in greedily, as if someone is finally hungry for all of her. Sarah recognizes with a sudden bolt of relief that she doesn't have to pretend, in his presence, that she has the remotest idea what will happen next.

She can let go with Tom because he is one of the wounded, he has lost something precious and irreplaceable that left a crater where his heart used to be. She feels his pain like a presence in the room with them, expanding and contracting with their breathing. The force of his loss flattens her to the bed sometimes, pressing into her like the aftershock from a nuclear explosion. It is the only time she feels alive, in the moments right after they have been in bed together.

She plots her time so that she can be alone with him. For a month, they manage to find each other, in K-mart shopping for back-to-school supplies with Zach and Maddie, on the boardwalk one evening, at the farm more than once. On Thursday, the first day of school, when it is nearly 3:20 and Sarah is scraping Elmer's glue off of the tabletops in her empty classroom, Tom comes up behind her with a basket of purple and yellow pansies for her windowsill. They close the door and for a foolish minute, kiss frantically in the darkened, humid room. Sarah is startled by how readily she clings to Tom and nuzzles her face against his shirt, straightens his collar afterward with a swift, wifely gesture. If Rose suspects anything, she is expert at keeping it a secret; she only wishes them both a warm "Good afternoon" as they walk together past her desk and out the front door.

Sarah goes home to Row with her knees still quivering, her heart rocketing dangerously. She is powerless to explain what is happening to her. She is not deluded enough to imagine that it is love; she loves her husband, after all, and her life. This is something more basic than love, some primary reckoning with fate that she cannot easily put an end to. Someone has changed all of the rules of her life overnight, and suddenly, she is no longer sure who or what she is supposed to be following.

Zach has started kindergarten in Ms. Verde's class, and he sobs every day before school. "I don't want to go to school, I hate it!" he moans sleepily, even before his eyes are fully open. He lies splayed on his bed like a puppy in the mornings, his arms and legs flopped out sideways on top of his blankets, and Sarah wants nothing more than to cover him up and let him fall back asleep, to tell him that it was all just a bad dream.

"Kindergarten is too hard," Zach protests after school one afternoon.

"What's hard, honey?" Sarah whispers, snuggling with him on the sofa. Zach looks at her as if she had suddenly taken leave of her senses. "Scissors, Mom," he explains in exasperation. "Scissors are hard, you're supposed to cut in a straight line. And lining up for recess! You're not allowed to talk at all, not for one second, even if Charlie Fitzer says something really, really funny!"

Now Sarah realizes, with only a small stab of guilt, that she is rushing Zach out the door each morning, hoping to catch a glimpse of Tom when he drops Maddie off at school. On the afternoons when Maddie isn't coming over to the studio for Art Club, Sarah even leaves her son in the after-care room at school so that she can drive out to the farm for two uninterrupted hours with Tom. They make love like two people stranded together in the desert. At those times only, she feels her grief about her father lift like a veil and hover, glimmering, above them. Afterwards, they sit out on Tom's front porch or lie on his bed and talk, about their children, about Lily and Sarah's father, never about Row. Until the veil descends again, and it is time to leave.

When Sarah nestles into her own bed at night it occurs to her that her night fears are gone; she no longer pictures burglars hiding behind the living room drapes, or imagines that she has left a door open somewhere that must be checked immediately. *If only someone had told me this was the cure*, she thinks drowsily, hugging her pillow and keeping her eyes shut so Row will think she is sleeping, *I would have considered infidelity years ago.*

She has avoided talking to Ginna for nearly a week, saying she is not feeling well and keeping busy with the beginning of the school year. Ginna seems, thankfully, too preoccupied with her own marriage to notice anything strange. She and Pat are preparing to go away for the weekend, on some kind of Catholic couples retreat.

Abby calls twice that week, and Sarah forces herself to push thoughts of Tom out of her mind. Their conversation is mainly about their father. The oncologist has warned them that swelling from the combined effects of the chemo and radiation might make it very difficult for him to eat normally, particularly in the months immediately after he finished chemo. Lately, Daddy is complaining that his neck and jaw hurt, and it is increasingly difficult for him to swallow.

Lynda reports that if she cuts his food into small pieces and mixes them with a lot of mashed potatoes, he is able to eat a little bit of solid food. She fixes elaborate dinners for him every day, his favorites, trying to entice him to eat: a standing rib roast one night, lamb chops the next, thick sirloin steaks on the grill with fried potatoes on Fridays.

"So what's the plan?" Abby asks dryly when Sarah reports the details of their father's latest meals. "Blow his arteries out quick, before the cancer has a chance to get him?"

They both laugh, a little too wildly and a little too long, say "I love you," and hang up. Neither of them says, "Do you think . . ?" but they end the conversation, for once, without mentioning the latest trial of a new drug that one of them has located on a cancer website. None of the doctors have spoken the word "remission." Remission, in fact, is entirely unlikely with this type of cancer. And yet Sarah hangs up the phone that night feeling like the world might not be crashing down around her ears. At least not immediately. She fixes herself a huge butterscotch sundae with Breyer's French vanilla ice cream and whipped topping from a spray can, the kind that is loaded with chemicals, and eats it slowly and deliberately, thinking how good it is to eat exactly as much ice cream as you really want.

Sarah's mother and Hen both call during the week, too, and Sarah is seized with the need to ask them questions like "Are you afraid of dying?" and "Have you ever had an affair?" Instead, they chat about the weather, politics, and their daily activities. Sarah's mother is thinking of taking a trip with her book club to Las Vegas. Hen went to the beauty parlor today, only to discover that her "regular girl" wasn't there.

"I don't know how these girls keep their jobs," Hen says in disgust. "Always taking a day off here, a day off there. I had to have

Diane do my hair and wait till you see it, she gave me a poof on top of my head. It's just ridiculous. I'm an old woman, what do I want with a poof?"

Sarah does not mention that she has been to the beauty salon herself this week, to have her hair styled and to get a pedicure, something she rarely indulges in. Tom noticed the new softness of her feet immediately, grasping her insteps in his hands as soon as they were alone in bed, placing his mouth over her newly-polished toes, and tickling until she collapsed with laughter. It makes her shudder to remember his hands on her body. If Rowland notices any change, Sarah thinks, he is probably relieved, taking it as a sign that she is "coming out of her gloom," as he calls it, and taking better care of herself.

I am taking better care of myself, Sarah thinks. She is sitting in the window seat sipping a second glass of wine. She stares around her kitchen, the bright yellow placemats and the basket of oranges placed neatly on the table, Zach's drawing of a castle on the refrigerator. He had drawn it at summer camp, a big, lopsided castle with a family of dolphins swimming happily around the castle moat, each one with a big blue crayon smile. Sarah is grateful that this is the way her son sees the world, sunny and without menace. *Let it stay that way, please.*

Zach stopped her in the middle of making dinner last night to point to the eggplant lying side by side on the kitchen counter, impossibly purple-black and round. He grabbed them up in his arms and asked, "Mama, did you ever love a food so much you just had to run with it?" Sarah watched laughing as he tore around the kitchen, hugging two eggplants close to his chest like footballs, like something that could bring him glory.

She wanders over to the counter now, and her eyes rest on the eggplant, their glossy purple shine against the wooden bowl. She will not easily admit to anyone what she does next. She picks up a single eggplant, the largest one. It is surprisingly heavy, cool, and satisfying in her hands. Cradling the eggplant under her breasts the way Zach had, she waits for the impulse to run. She feels nothing, and then suddenly runs anyway, in big dancing circles around the dining room table, her feet in sandals clapping so loudly and for so long on the tile floor that Connie, asleep in the next room, jumps up and stumbles in groggily to see what on earth is happening.

Afterwards, tumbled into a kitchen chair, panting, she feels ridiculous. She returns the eggplant to its place in the bowl, careful to re-position it exactly, as if someone passing by might notice that it had temporarily gone missing.

Something about the eggplant's surprising heft, its roundness and the thick, tight skin stays with Sarah for the rest of the day. Not glory, certainly. But there is something: a memory of that deep, lush purple and the sun in the fields that once warmed it. A pleasant tingling along her arms, the way you feel after holding a baby for a long while, or something else tender and important.

Stan

He believes Millie can stop his cancer. Stan pours a second glass of wine for Millie and looks into her eyes and believes she just might be able to halt this thing in its tracks. She is smiling at him, and he has an urge to ask her to please put up her hand—his own personal traffic cop—as a signal to the rogue cells that their time is up. Finito. He has heard of foods with a high concentration of certain substances—antioxidants—that can inhibit the growth of cancer cells. If blueberries could hold such power, why not a person? Why not this particular person with her deep blue eyes and her absolute faith that Stan was cut out for greatness?

He usually goes to the office for a few hours on Mondays after chemo, but today is different. Today Millie reminded him that it was the 35th anniversary of the passage of the Mine Safety Act, the bill they had worked so hard for, together. So they are sitting in a café on Lexington Avenue near Stan's apartment, waiting for lunch menus and drinking a toast to the coal miners of Farmington, West Virginia, who had started them on the long road to finally passing a law to protect workers' safety. Stan remembers Jacob Javits giving one of the best speeches of his career in the Senate chamber, railing against the coal industry and its injustices.

"You were always the Senator's right hand man," Millie is saying emphatically. "Everyone knew how much he trusted you. That bill never could have passed without you there giving him the ammunition he needed to fight for it."

Stan is absolutely focused on Millie in that moment, the sun glancing off her hair and making her squint slightly, the way her fingers play with her fork. He raises his glass and leans in toward the center of their table. Millie bends toward him and her warm breath touches his skin. He can feel her breath healing him and the sun on his face and the cancer cells in his throat receding and his strength returning, flowing through his arms and legs. He closes his eyes.

"Daddy!" Stan opens his eyes in confusion and looks up into the face of his daughter. Sarah stands on the sidewalk by their table, a purse and her overnight bag slipping slowly from her shoulder. He remembers now: Lynda scheduled an appointment for all of them tomorrow with a family therapist at the hospital, someone that the oncologist recommended. Sarah had decided to come a day early and stay overnight with them in New York. Abby will undoubtedly be arriving soon, too. For some reason, everyone seems convinced that it is necessary for Stan and his family to talk about his illness, when all Stan needs to talk about is how he is feeling healthier by the minute.

"Hi, honey." He smiles and starts to rise abruptly, bumping the table and spilling red wine. Sarah stares at the stain spreading on the tablecloth. Somehow, in the time it takes Stan to get to his feet and clumsily begin to blot up the wine spill, Millie has slipped away, sparing him an awkward explanation for their lunch. Stan glances down Lexington Avenue and thinks he sees Millie's back disappearing into the 86th Street subway station, tries to hide the sense of loss that pierces him. *My daughter is a pain in the ass*, he thinks; and simultaneously feels like a teenager caught having sex in his parents' bedroom.

Sarah

"You need to see your father cry," Ginna says.

Sarah looks up, startled. "What?" Ginna has come over for an early morning cup of coffee before Sarah leaves for Union Station. She is booked on the 9 a.m. Metroliner to New York. Her friend stands next to her on the back patio, stirring sugar into her coffee.

"Well, really, Sarah. Don't you need him to show you that he's sad? That his heart is broken because he isn't going to be there for Zach's bar mitzvah, or for the rest of your life?" Ginna is looking at her from behind a pair of oval black sunglasses. Sarah admires the glasses briefly. She could use a pair like that.

"I think," she says carefully, "that all of that Catholic counseling is melting your brain."

Sarah hasn't seen her father cry in twenty-seven years, not since the girls' mother walked out the door. That night, their father held the two of them, Abby and Sarah, tight against him, his red flannel shirt damp with sweat, a half-full pack of Lucky Strikes crushed in the front pocket. She never wants to see anyone sob like that again.

She calls her mother from the train station, impulsively, and tries to explain. "He's dying, Mom. I don't know what I'm supposed to

do. He's dwindling away to nothing. He can't even speak anymore —
his voice is almost gone—and he and Lynda are just pretending that
he's going to get better."

"Well, whose fault is that?" her mother asks after a small
silence. "I mean, I guess all those years of smoking finally caught up
with him."

Sarah stares at the phone in her hand. "What did you just say?"

There is a sigh at the other end of the line. "It's not like he
didn't know the cigarettes would eventually kill him, honey."

Sarah shrieks into the phone. "You are officially off my list of
people I call when I need support! Off. My. List."

Now she sits across from her father in the family therapist's tiny,
cramped office at Sloan-Kettering, just down the hall from the room
where he comes for chemo. They have gathered for a meeting at the
suggestion of the oncologist. It can't be a good sign if your therapist seems
nervous, Sarah thinks. Mark Pachter shifts in his chair and fidgets with a
pencil, waiting for them to find chairs and settle in, arrange their jackets,
purses and notepads. "Why don't we begin," he says, "by telling me about
where you are in your treatment. You are undergoing chemotherapy now,
is that right, Mr. Gershman?"

Where we are is that my father is dying, Sarah thinks ferociously. *We
need to know how to prepare for this, what to do, what to expect.* But instead of
talking about that, they spend the next thirty minutes reviewing all of her

father's symptoms and appointments, discussing pain medication, the pros and cons of radiation, the apparent success of the chemotherapy, the grim survival statistics. Although the chemo has worked so far, her father's oncologist has advised them that it is just a matter of time—maybe only months—before the tumors begin to grow again. Sarah has memorized the bleak statistics: less than fifty percent of patients with this kind of cancer survive five years. And her father's tumors, the doctors keep reminding them, are "particularly aggressive." *Macho, macho tumors*, Sarah and Abby called them on the phone one night, giggling guiltily.

She looks at her father, thinks about that odd moment, finding him at the café. She pushes away the image of him blotting red wine from the tablecloth and not meeting her eyes.

Dr. Pachter asks them each in turn to say a bit about their lives, and how they are feeling. There is a long moment when they all look around the room, uncertainty building in the air. For as long as Sarah can remember, her father has been the force moving the family forward, and as he sits in his chair now, resolutely silent, they all seem a little pathetic to her, adrift without his lead. Lynda, Sarah and Abby speak up eventually, and talk about stress and daily anxiety. "It's like living on a roller coaster," Abby admits softly. "You never know when the up times are coming, and you can never prepare for the downs." Lynda mentions how difficult it is for her to take time off work for all of the doctors' appointments. After the therapist looks at Sarah's father patiently, for a long moment, Daddy says he is feeling a bit tired from the constant fevers, but hopeful.

"It's clear to me that you are a very close family," Dr. Pachter is saying, crossing his legs carefully. "And that you find it easy to talk to each other. But I can also see some work that is left to do, some areas that haven't been touched on yet."

Sarah waits expectantly. Across from her, her father raises his eyebrows, gives the therapist a dubious look.

"People in your situation are often thinking about their legacy, about what they want to leave behind," Dr. Pachter continues. "They are sometimes planning their funerals. So I'm wondering, have you talked with your family about the kind of funeral you'd like to have, Mr. Gershman?"

Sarah nods her head. She has imagined the funeral several different ways: sometimes she is wearing black, sometimes the dark purple silk suit that she wore to Deb Rosen's daughter's bat mitzvah. In one version of the event, Sarah is calm and composed, able to walk up to the podium and address the group of friends and relatives, to speak gracefully and lovingly about her father's life. In another version she cannot talk at all, to anyone, throughout the entire service or the graveside *Kaddish*. She does not know how to begin to compress an entire life into a five-minute speech; it is too much for anyone to expect that she should select what is remembered and what will be assigned to oblivion. Every time she tries to imagine the words she might say, she pictures herself tottering on high heels near the gravesite, the ground shivering around her when she tries to walk. The headstones in the cemetery sway precariously.

Her father is shaking his head. "No," he manages to whisper, his finger covering the hole in his trach tube, speaking slowly and deliberately, "Not giving it much thought." He coughs, chokes, turns to his pad in frustration and starts to write, Abby reading the words aloud as he scribbles them: "I want to go on with my life. Want everything to feel normal."

The writing tablets her father uses have become smaller, Sarah notices. In the beginning, his words sprawled boldly across the pages of yellow legal pads, often running right off the page. Lately, he seems content to reach for the red spiral notebooks that Lynda buys and leaves around the apartment for him. He is writing now in cramped letters on a tiny memo pad, smaller than the one Sarah bought for Zach to carry to kindergarten.

"Daddy," Sarah begins slowly, "If I knew I was going to die, I think I would be thinking a lot about what I wanted to say to Zach, what I could leave him with. Do you think about that, what you want to say to us?" Her voice quivers and she hates herself for it, focuses on ripping up a Kleenex in her lap so she will not have to look up at her father's face.

"No," he writes on his pad, pressing so hard that the edges of the paper shake. "Haven't thought much about it." Silence falls in the room after he finishes.

"What do you think about?" Sarah asks hotly. She feels brutish, unkind for pursuing this when her father clearly doesn't want to. Her earnestness is lost on him; he is no longer meeting her gaze. "It doesn't seem like you've made plans to do anything differently, even if you might not—you know, if we don't know how much time you have left." Sarah has now made a nest of shredded tissues in her lap.

"Work as long as I can," he answers, writing rapidly. "Spend as much time as we can in Vermont this summer. Beyond that, nothing special. Want life to feel normal," he repeats, underlining the last word.

"But it's not normal!" Sarah begins to cry into a fresh Kleenex. "Tell me what's normal about cancer?" No one answers her. Abby is nodding, tears in her eyes, but says nothing.

"I know you don't want to think about what is going to happen. But maybe you have to, Daddy, for us."

"Well." The therapist breaks in, his voice gentle. "It seems clear that each member of the family is experiencing things very differently. Mr. Gershman, you are focused on how to go on with your life, while your daughters, and perhaps your wife?" with an inquiring look at Lynda, who has fallen silent, "They are preparing to lose you, trying to say good-bye, which is entirely understandable."

Her father shrugs, turns almost imperceptibly in his seat, taps one hand against his leg as if he is bored. He will not look at either his daughters or his wife. He does not say anything more for the remainder of the session. As they shake hands with Dr. Pachter and walk out the door Sarah stares at her father's back, the round and resolute crest of his shoulders, the way his body seems to draw into itself and stand alone despite the bright flurry of his family around him, despite Lynda's arm linked firmly through his. Sarah and Abby pause in the reception area and hug, standing together for a long moment with their arms entwined. They talk about their travel plans, and discuss having a cup of coffee before they go their separate ways. Abby reaches up to wipe a tear from Sarah's cheek. Their father, meanwhile, has slipped hastily away from them, without a word, and is walking toward the street to hail a cab. Lynda follows behind, leaving his two daughters stunned, watching their father through the hospital window as he climbs into the cab with a hasty wave over his shoulder.

It doesn't matter, Sarah realizes on the long train ride home. Good memories or bad, a long good-bye or a quick wave from the curb, it makes no difference if I hate him or love him, he is still going to die. And he will die the way he wants to, with or without my blessing.

She knows that Row and Ginna have begun whispering about her again, furtively comparing notes, treating her as if she is on the verge of splintering. Perhaps she is falling apart; she has alienated her family, she has cheated on her husband, she has embarrassed herself in front of colleagues at school. God knows she should pull herself together. Everyone else is managing, all of the people in the Amtrak station and in the neighborhoods fleeting by her window—they wake up and pour milk over their children's breakfast cereal, decide whether to wear the brown pumps or the black, climb into their cars and put keys into the ignition with perfect faith that their engines will start and another day will begin to roll forward very much as the previous one did. They do all this, perhaps sensing only dimly that at any moment it could all be snatched away.

When the train stops at Union Station, Sarah gets off the train and does not call Row on her cell phone. She drives the thirty-five miles to the Chesapeake Bay in silence, then parks her car near the boardwalk in North Beach and walks down to the water's edge. It is Sarah's favorite time to be on the Bay, the hour before sunset when the clouds thicken to a smoky blue, and the line where sky meets the slow curve of the water blurs, growing steadily dimmer and dimmer. A few stray sailboats far out at the northern end of the Bay, headed home to Annapolis or Baltimore, catch the sun's light and gleam startling pink against the darkening horizon. It is a time when the air appears deeper than it really is, when a person gazing across the shining water might believe she was seeing all the way out to the Atlantic Ocean, not just eleven miles across to Tilghman Island, as the wooden plaque mounted above the boardwalk railing explains.

Sarah craves this view whenever she has been away from home. The particular rose-colored light thrown across the Bay by the disappearing sun, the expanse of shimmering water. The knowledge of fish gathering beneath the waves, their slick, dark bodies circling close to the surface, quivering in anticipation of the evening's hunt for food. She will stay here staring at the water until it is no longer possible to see, until the deep blue-gray of the sky is indistinguishable from the waves below. Until the ending of one thing and the beginning of another look the same; and the enormous effort of trying to discern one from the other leads nowhere.

Part Three

Stan

The glacier jiggles like jello, then fractures as Stan watches, into a million crystalline pieces. Ice melts and becomes a heaving ocean with piercing sunlight overhead. And far below, the massive, shadowy bodies of whales hover, suspended beneath the water's surface. He is down in the shadows with them now, swimming, feeling keenly the presence of another region somewhere close by, a place that he doesn't quite recognize.

He opens his mouth and expects to taste the ocean. Instead, sound flows out: his voice. Stan has never understood this before, how his throat forms a perfect cylindrical tunnel leading directly to his heart and lungs, to the breath that fills his airways and swells his chest. He begins to sing along with the whales, and he thinks they are bellowing out an aria from La Traviata, the final scene where Violetta succumbs to her illness. The last thing Stan thinks before salt water floods his lungs is: I'm sorry, Mother.

First it is Wednesday, then it is suddenly Friday afternoon, and Stan has no recollection of anything passing in between. He wakes up in a hospital bed and experiences a wave of panic, wondering if the cancer has finally gotten him. He presses the nurses' call button again and again. "Am I dying?" he demands of the sleepy male nurse who finally walks into the room. Once they realize he is awake there is a sudden flurry of activity—Stan is hooked up to monitors and IV bags, and still nobody is telling him what the hell happened.

The psychiatrist who comes to see him two hours later doesn't help clarify the situation. She is young, attractive, and in Stan's opinion, wears her skirts far too short. "Patients can't stop thinking about your legs," he writes with a smile. He almost crosses it out after he writes it, but he hands the notebook to her, thinking it must be the morphine making him bold.

"Mr. Gershman." The lady psychiatrist clears her throat and crosses her spectacular legs. Tanned, as if she has just returned from a tropical vacation. "It would help if you could tell me the last thing you remember before you woke up today in the hospital," she says smoothly. Stan thinks hard and remembers only whales, a dream of swimming underneath a dark blue glacier. If he tells her about that, she is definitely going to think he's ready for the loony bin. He shakes his head sheepishly. "Can't remember anything," he scrawls with his pen.

Lynda is the one who finally tells him that he took too many pain pills, and very nearly died. Stan is dumbstruck. His wife is looking at him in desperation, willing him to say he didn't mean it, and he wonders whether or not he had. Sometimes the pain is relentless enough, and his fears dark enough, to make him wish it were all over.

The psychiatrist comes back, and asks him question after question: Is he depressed? "Only morons have cancer & are not depressed," Stan scribbles, looking at her sharply. But suicidal? No.

Gone Bolshevik

Does he remember taking the pain pills? Does he believe he is dying? What does he believe in? Stan believes fervently in two things: love and reason. One has absolutely nothing to do with the other—after two divorces, Stan should know that better than anybody. And yet he has faith in them both: in reason to help us make sense of the world, and in love—well, to make it worth being alive, and to enjoy showing up day after day. So no, he does not want to die yet, he tells Lynda emphatically, and he repeats the same thing to the pretty psychiatrist until she is convinced—finally—to let him go home.

Stan can imagine the dumb animal part of himself voting for oblivion, if that meant an escape from the pain. But what he can't understand is why his rational brain hadn't kicked in to save him. It makes him skittish around himself, unsure every time he pops a pill into his mouth. He can see from the expressions on his wife and daughters' faces that they are anxious, too. He has been watching for any signs that his mind was losing the upper hand—when that happens, he thinks, just shoot me. But unless he has missed something, he is still firmly *compis mentis*.

He is not sure whether it's the animal or rational part of himself that packs an overnight bag and takes the subway to Millie's apartment. Her face crumples when she sees him, and when he explains what happened it is the first time she has lost her composure in front of him. "Oh, Stan," she keeps saying, and finally presses her lilac-scented cheek into his shoulder, her face damp against his collarbone. When she invites him inside Stan is completely sure that for once, he is doing exactly the right thing.

Stan knows that to most people he would seem like a cliché: the middle-aged man chasing after his secretary. But those people would be wrong. For starters, she hasn't been his secretary for nearly twenty-five years, since he worked for the Senate. And for seconds, Millie is not the type to become someone's girl on the side. She takes herself very seriously; she always has. When he lets her fold him into her arms and tells her he loves her Stan is serious, too.

Sarah

A lab technician is attaching electrodes to her son's scalp, and Sarah is practicing her deep yoga breathing. This particular test, to determine whether Zach is experiencing seizures or other erratic brain waves, must be performed when the patient is asleep. Sarah was instructed to deprive Zach of sleep for 12 hours, which she did, and then she drove him here, cranky and weeping, to be hooked up to some kind of brain wave detector. This technician has absolutely no skill with children, and is becoming irritated because Zach keeps pulling the electrodes off his head. Luckily, Zach thinks the machine is interesting, so Sarah is able to distract him by pointing to the squiggly jellyfish waves moving up and down on the screen, while she rubs his belly and talks to him in a soothing voice.

"Mama?" Zach is on the edge of sleep, his head lolling to one side, orange plastic wires criss-crossing his hair. His scalp is wet with sweat.

"What, sweet pea?"

"Why can't I hear God talk?"

Before Sarah can think of an answer, Zach lifts his head with a huge, sleepy smile to look at her, tugging off a yellow wire. The lab technician makes an exasperated sound, which Sarah ignores.

Zach is regarding her seriously now. "I think we need to have a different kind of ears, that's all. Then we could hear God talking to us, just like Abraham did."

Sarah nods. "I wish we had those ears, don't you?" She kisses her son's damp head and slowly, reluctantly, he allows himself to be settled against the pillow. She blows the hair away from his face and resumes rubbing his belly. After what seems like an eternity, Zach's eyelids drop closed and he falls asleep.

Sarah is sure that the test will be negative. She knows that her son is more sensitive than most kids to sounds and smells, but she considers this an intense awareness, a gift. She is convinced that she, too, has been existing in an altered state lately, her own senses made keener, sharpened by the awareness of death close at hand. Like animals on a hunt, she explains to Ginna, running in circles because they are already picking up the scent of blood. Or Betazoids, Ginna reminds her with a smile.

The neurologist who meets with Sarah a week later is very reassuring. All of Zach's tests came back normal. "I suspect that what you're seeing here is a mild form of synesthesia," Dr. Wooster explains smoothly. "That's simply a heightened sensitivity, so that the way Zach takes in the sensory world is different. In your son's case, there seems to be a powerful link between sounds and color, or smells and color. Zach actually sees sounds and smells as visual images projected in space in front of him, like a movie."

Sarah is listening and nodding. It makes perfect sense—it fits with the way Zach seems to be overwhelmed in loud places, and his funny way of connecting sounds and smells with color. "He once told me that Monday smelled like red."

Dr. Wooster nods. "That's right, he probably confuses sound, smell, and color sometimes, because they all merge in his perception."

"So when he was stuck on the slide that day at school . . .?" Sarah asks.

"On the top of the slide, the noises of his surrounding environment—bird calls, the rustling of leaves, kids yelling below, you name it—all of those sounds became like a movie of sliding shapes in the air all around Zach. In kids his age, that can lead to a kind of sensory overload that is paralyzing, so they shut down momentarily."

"So is he always going to go on overload this way?" Sarah asks.

"I can't tell you exactly when, but he will most likely grow out of it." Dr. Wooster points to a diagram of the human brain hanging on the wall of her office. "As Zach grows up and his visual and auditory cortexes continue to develop, these episodes of sensory overload should become less and less frequent. The brain has an amazing capacity to adapt. Zach's brain is constantly re-calibrating, based on repeated experiences in his life."

We are both on sensory overload, Sarah thinks on the drive home. And it's not a gift, it's a curse. Row doesn't seem to get overwhelmed the way she does—maybe because he simply perceives the world exactly the way it is, without distortion. For Sarah, like her son, there is always an overwhelming amount of information flooding in, liquid and uncontainable.

She imagines her brain the way Dr. Wooster described it: sifting through an intricate web of stimuli, minute by minute, to decide which bits of sensory information require attention and which ones can be jettisoned. How efficient if we could only control the pruning process. She thinks of the way illness draws us into a heightened physical awareness of each other, how when she is near her father now she is flooded with the sour tang of his sweat and the earthy, fertile odor of decay that rises from his mouth. She does not want to smell this, does not want to be aware of the way her father's body is slowly composting itself from the inside out. Really, why couldn't her brain edit that part out? Those are definitely things a daughter does not want to remember.

Stan

First Lucky Strike and first feel of a girl's tit: the plan was to achieve them both by age 14. Stan and his best friend George made a pact. The Lucky Strikes were no problem; George's older brother smoked, and it wasn't difficult to steal a few cigarettes here and there. They ran into the woods in back of George's house and lit up, pretending they knew what they were doing. It took three matches before George could get a cigarette lit, and then the boys drew in the pungent smoke, coughing almost immediately. The hot smoke filled Stan's throat and made him feel like he was going to throw up, but it was glorious—the burn, the feel of the cigarette dangling from his lips. Stan decided he loved everything about Lucky Strikes: the way the smoke curled up from the end of the cigarette and into the air, the way when he inhaled, heat bit into his lungs and rushed straight to his brain, making him feel light-headed and more keenly aware of everything around him.

He loved the girls in the Lucky Strike magazine ads, too, posed in the front seat of a slick Buick convertible or lying on the beach, smoking in the sun. *Be Happy, Go Lucky!* His mother's friends in Miami lounged in plastic chairs outside their cabanas, smoking, and imagined they looked like the magazine ads, cigarettes in one manicured hand

and drinks in the other.

It took Stan two summers in Miami before he found a girl on the beach who would let him touch her. Three weeks after Robbie died, his father announced that Stan was going to move to Florida with his mother. "Miami Beach!" he proclaimed loudly, as if that explained everything. "Just for a while, it will be fun." They packed up and moved into a small apartment on Collins Avenue, with a view of the ocean.

Stan hated the beach, forced himself to go there every morning just to get out of the apartment. His mother slept late, and once she was awake she locked herself in the bathroom for an hour, running a bath and smoking, drinking her first cup of coffee. Around noon, she went downstairs to the cabana, and Stan was left alone. If he stayed in the apartment, he was only allowed to open the door for the Jehovah's Witnesses or Mrs. Cutler, who lived next door. He liked Mrs. Cutler; she baked him cake and almond rugelach. But he started to feel pathetic, hanging out alone in an apartment waiting for an old lady to bring him rugelach. So after the first month, Stan struck out on his own, slipping quietly out of the apartment every morning to walk on the beach.

He detested the sand, the way it clung to his swim trunks and scraped the insides of his legs. By about eleven, the sand was too hot to walk on, so Stan kept close to the water's edge, kicking his feet in the shallow surf, walking without knowing where he was headed. The girl saw him before he spotted her; by the time Stan raised his eyes from the water, squinting, and noticed the blonde girl in the aquamarine bathing suit walking toward him, she was already staring at him. She glanced away quickly, pretending to look at the waves lapping at her feet. All he took in as they walked past each other was her bathing suit: bright blue and a two-piece, without straps on top. She had nice shoulders.

"Nice shoulders?!" George said when Stan described her, scandalized. "That's what you noticed?" Truthfully, Stan didn't have time to see anything else; but something about the girl stayed with him, and he found himself looking for her on his morning walks.

The next time he saw her, she asked him for a cigarette, and Stan fell instantly in love. Her name was Rita. She was older than he was—fifteen—and he could tell by the way she held her Lucky Strike while he fumbled with the matches, struggling to keep one lit in the wind, that she knew what she was doing. They kissed on their first date—if you could call a walk on the beach a date, which Stan believed you could. Still, he was stunned when, a week later, Rita took his sweaty hand and placed it firmly on her bathing suit top. They were sitting on the sand near the construction site for a new hotel, smoking and watching a giant crane rise against the sky. Stan left his hand there, just slightly above where the fabric of her top gathered and dipped down, feeling the warmth of the sun on her skin and the slight swell of her left breast beneath his fingers, not sure what his next move was supposed to be. This isn't the way he would report the scene to George the following day; in Stan's retelling, he was the one who took the lead. He looked into Rita's eyes, instead of staring stupidly past her at the construction site, where an enormous mound of earth had been moved to lay the foundation for the hotel. After what felt like an eternity, Stan let his hand brush gently over Rita's bathing suit and drop to his side.

They left Miami a month later, his mother having finally

decided she was ready to return to New York, and Stan never saw Rita again. But the smells of the ocean and the grit of sand forever brought back that summer to him—both the thrill of warm skin and the painful awareness that Stan had no idea what he was meant to do next.

He feels exactly the same way now. If George were here, Stan could easily make up another story to explain why he is sitting in Millie's apartment this morning sipping coffee while she showers in the next room and while his wife is undoubtedly frantic to know where he is and what the hell he thinks he is doing. Stan feels stupid, slow, and completely unsure of what comes next—and yet also somehow more keenly alive than he has felt in a very long time.

Sarah

I think I'm going crazy," Sarah says softly to Row one night when he walks in the door from work. "I went into the drugstore and almost bought a pack of Lucky Strikes, just so I could smell my father."

Row's mouth crinkles slightly and he turns away from her to open the hall closet. "My God, Sarah, don't tell me you're going to take up smoking." Concern laces his words; he is missing the point entirely. "That's what's killing him." Sarah watches her husband hang up his jacket as if he were a rare specimen she has never noticed before, one of the Brazilian beetles that Pats gets so excited about. *If he comes over here I will squash him,* she thinks coolly. *Like a bug.*

She calls Tom that night after Rowland has gone to bed, her hand hovering over the telephone for a long time before she dials. The phone rings ten times and then eleven, and then she hangs up quickly, her breath ragged. *Tell me about picking up your wife's clothes and smelling them,* she wants to say, leaning her face into his neck. *Tell me.*

Tom had handed her one of Lily's nightgowns last week, purple silk with spaghetti straps. He trailed it across the bed where Sarah lay, tickling her bare belly. Sarah scrupulously steers around Lily's things when she is in the house. She does not pick up photographs or books and ask about them; she avoids using any of the mugs in the kitchen cupboard that look especially feminine, or the ones with slogans like "Sisters are branches of the same tree." But when Tom held out the purple nightgown some impulse made Sarah reach for it and slip it on. She turned her back to Tom then and let him stroke the gown on her, let him run his mouth over every inch of it as if he were trying to suck the fabric into his own body, getting rougher and rougher as he moved over her. When they made love he grabbed her hips and squeezed so fiercely that she had red marks on her skin for days.

Sarah wonders now, fleetingly, whether Tom would smoke a Lucky Strike for her, if she asked him to.

The two of them are curled together in his bed when Sarah hears the rumble of a truck coming up the long driveway. "Tom!" It is 3:15 on a Saturday, and somehow they have both fallen asleep, allowing themselves the luxury of an afternoon nap. Stupid, stupid.

Stumbling out of bed in a panic, they pull on clothes. Two brown socks, two earrings. Aunt Kay is in the driveway, dropping Maddie off. A few more minutes, Sarah realizes with a sick feeling, and Tom's daughter would have run into the bedroom and found them.

Kay steps into the house and hugs Tom warmly. "I thought I'd come by and pick Maddie up tomorrow morning, take her to the bazaar at the church," she explains. She sees Sarah then, and hesitates for only a millisecond before recovering and smiling at her. "Hello there!" Carefully,

Kay turns to look at Tom.

"Sarah was just bringing by some art supplies for Maddie," Tom said. He is a poor liar, and Sarah can see at once that Kay knows. Sarah says her good-byes and rushes out the door. She can feel Tom's eyes on her as she climbs into her car and drives away, and she knows, too, that she has let this man fall a little bit in love with her. He will get over it, she tells herself, steering down the bumpy driveway. He will live for a while jumping when the teacups rattle, like his PTSD patients. But he will get over it.

"What do you mean, he's GONE?" Sarah yells into the phone. Lynda explains again, reads her father's cryptic note: *So sorry sweetie, but I need to be alone for a while.* Sarah has the irrational thought that her father has finally decided to kill himself, that maybe the last attempt had been half-hearted, but this one is for real. And yet she can't truly imagine her father giving up.

Where would he go? None of it is making any sense, until Sarah thinks again of finding her father in the café on Lexington Avenue. She knows he needs to slip away sometimes, and she suspects that he has found a coffee shop somewhere, a place where he can sit and the waitress will refill his coffee all morning, where nobody requires him to talk or asks any questions. Lynda, Sarah believes, tends to get a bit hysterical. *He needs you to laugh with him,* she wants to say to her father's wife. *To drink gin & tonics and not notice when he winces from the pain of swallowing. He needs you to look at him like he's not dead yet.* She hangs up without saying any of this to Lynda.

Something about the scene in the café lingers in Sarah's imagination. Her father had been going on and on about his secretary from the Senate days, Millie. His entire face relaxed when he talked about those days.

It is early morning in New Mexico. Sarah calls her mother and she answers on the first ring, surprised.

"Mom, I need to ask you something important, and please don't lie to me." Sarah says quickly.

"Okay." Her mother's voice is guarded.

"Remember Millie, from Dad's office? I think they had an affair."

"Sarah." There is a long pause. "That's ancient history."

Sarah says nothing, holds the phone in stony silence, and eventually her mother relents. "OK, yes, I knew your dad had a thing with Millie. And maybe we should have broken up then. Maybe we would have." There is another long pause, and Sarah's brain clicks into overdrive. *We would have – except for what?*

"When was this, Mom?"

Her mother sighs. "Back when Abby was little. A long time ago, Sarah. You weren't even born yet."

"Oh my God, you stayed together just because you got pregnant with me! Didn't you?"

When her mother speaks again her voice is even and careful. "Someday you're going to realize that everything doesn't revolve around you, sweetie. Life is more complicated than that. We stayed together because we were married, and we loved each other, and that's what you did back then."

Gone Bolshevik

Sarah hangs up the phone, stung. Great, more guilt to heap on top of everything she's already feeling. More evidence that her family is not what she believed it was, that the ground under her feet is shaky. She is on the verge of picking up the phone again, to tell Ginna or Abby, but she hesitates. She thinks of her father, spending his life trying hard to do the right thing. Marrying his pregnant girlfriend because that's what a young man was expected to do. She sees him in their old blue Plymouth station wagon, driving his wife and daughters down the highway, his hands proud and sure on the wheel. Or out on his sailboat, navigating (with mixed results) the waters of the Patuxent. Finding his way through three turbulent marriages. He has tried to be the family compass for his entire life, and maybe now it's his time to let go, to acknowledge that things have gone haywire, that the magnetic field is no longer holding true.

Stan

The reptile eye is always there, blinking, behind our human eye. Sometimes, Stan realizes, you can manage to lull it to sleep.

The trip here was arduous, much more complicated than he imagined. Stan needed supplies – he hadn't packed enough saline solution or vanilla Peptamen in his hurry to get out of the apartment. By the time they found a drugstore that sold everything he needed, Stan was exhausted and slept all the way to the airport.

When Stan's trach tube set off the metal detector, a young airport security officer told him he would have to take the tube out. Although it would be painful, Stan was ready to comply, but Millie was adamantly set against it.

"You are asking this man to remove a part of his body," she pointed out, stepping in front of Stan to give the young officer the full force of her stare—which, Stan knew, could be daunting. "What if he had an artificial limb? Would he need to remove that, too?"

"Ma'am," the security officer attempted, "We do sometimes require passengers to remove a prosthetic device, yes—I mean, if it can be easily taken off…."

"That's not the point at all," Millie said smoothly, and Stan watched the young man's face cloud in momentary confusion. "The point is, he requires that tube to breathe and to swallow, and I'm quite sure there is a REGULATION against asking a passenger to stop breathing, don't you think?"

Stan thought that wasn't entirely accurate, but he had to admire her spunk. The security officer backed down, and soon they were settling in to their seats at the gate. On the plane, Stan asked for gin, and the flight attendant was a little horrified to see him reach under his shirt to pour the gin into his stomach tube. Millie was Millie—she took everything in her stride, but Stan is beginning to worry that the situation is wearing down even her remarkable reserves of grace. He resolves not to fall asleep on the plane; he doesn't want Millie to see the copious amounts of drool his mouth produces, and he's sure it will drip down onto the new white golf shirt he put on this morning. But the five-hour flight is too much for him and he is soon fast asleep.

They are standing at the South Rim of the Grand Canyon, and Stan can't believe he actually made it. He gazes out over the stunning, wide open expanse, feels in the pit of his stomach what it would be like to simply let go and fall over the edge, to soar into all of that yawning space. The wind up here is fierce today, and he is happy for that—for once the roaring outside his head is louder than the roaring inside.

Stan is in the wind. It gusts all around him and blows through him, as if his legs have become stone, embedded in the canyon walls.

He stands rooted on the red dirt shelf with his arms lifted, letting the wind whip the breath from his body so that he gasps, suddenly. Not in pain but with recognition. This is all I wanted, he sees now. To stand here and to calm the noise down for just a minute so I can think. And remember. The names of the canyon's rock layers come to him like a mantra: *Kaibab, Toroweap, Coconino, Hermit shale, Tapeats, Bright Angel shale.* Such luminous and hopeful names. He wants to call his daughters up and tell them where he is right now, to see if they, too, can remember.

Soon after he started dating Lynda, Stan had taken her and his teenaged daughters on a raft trip down the Colorado River. Five days deep in the Grand Canyon, eating and sleeping and waking to the thunderous rush of the river. They slept in tents on the river's narrow sandy beaches, and brushed their teeth every morning in frigid creek water. They learned to notice the signs of approaching rapids long before they could hear them, to spot the "V" shape in the river's current. In the hot afternoon hours, when they were not traveling on the raft, they explored side canyons and discovered hidden waterfalls. They memorized the names for each of the layers of rock that lined the canyon walls in exquisite ribbons of ochre, red, and brown.

At the end of the trip, they drove from the Canyon to Las Vegas, where they would spend one night in the MGM Grand Hotel and then catch a flight home in the morning. Lynda and Abby had dressed and hurried excitedly down to the lobby to shop and to play the slot machines, while Sarah stayed with Stan upstairs in their lavish, over-decorated hotel room. Stan can still remember touching the gleaming gold hot and cold water faucets in the bathroom sink, wondering why everything looked so bright and so hard. Sarah spent most of the evening in front of the window staring down over the extravagant lights of Las Vegas. Without needing to ask, he knew that his daughter missed the sound of the Colorado River rushing in her ears. He did, too.

I would be terrified to raft those rapids now, Stan realizes with a jolt. When did I get so afraid?

He tries to explain it to Millie at the airport, while they wait for their flight back to JFK. It is an awkward conversation, with Stan writing furiously on his notepad, and Millie reading over his shoulder, not saying much. "Needed to get out. Be surrounded by something bigger than myself. Bigger than all of us." Millie reads this and squeezes his hand. "I know, Stan."

"You know in the movies, when you see an old couple and they still love each other?" Stan is writing laboriously, wanting to get every word right. "Because they can remember when they were young & strong & beautiful & full of dreams?" he asks. "Lynda doesn't remember me. When I'm around her, I don't know myself sometimes. Being back here—now, I remember." Millie's lips are trembling only slightly as she reads his words.

When he finishes writing, Stan is afraid to look up at Millie, his one hook into some kind of sanity, his tonic to quiet the reptile brain and its impulses. She is reaching into her purse and takes out a comb, begins pulling it through her long frizzy hair—where he had rested his mouth just a day ago—then tosses her head once, a schoolgirl gesture that nearly makes him come undone, and pulls it back sharply into a ponytail. She is nothing if not full of grace and prepared for anything. Millie. He takes her hand, and she will not meet his eyes, and together they wait for their flight to be called.

Sarah

Her father and Lynda won't be coming to Sarah's house for Thanksgiving this year, and she is secretly relieved. Thanksgiving has never been one of her favorite holidays. Way too much time spent in the kitchen for too little return. Cranberry sauce stains on the tablecloth that never come out, and the huge, grotesque turkey carcass that Sarah always feels compelled to save because she is sure it will make a delicious soup stock. Every year she keeps it in the back of the fridge for a week or two until it begins to smell, and then she throws it out.

At least, she thinks, rubbing lemon oil into the grain of her dining room table, it is not a holiday she is used to spending with her father. Thanksgiving will still be hers, after he's gone. She remembers when Helene's mother died on June 21, the first day of summer, and Helene said it ruined summertime for her forever. Already Sarah can sense the slow paring away of her normal life, the perfectly ordinary things she will not be able to encounter without thinking of her father: Amtrak train stations, taxicabs, humidifiers, applesauce, notepads.

She has not talked to her father since he returned home. She refuses to call the apartment and hear Lynda's tired voice, her forced cheer when she knows it is Sarah on the line. Sarah is furious at her father and knows she has no right to be, and the knowledge paralyzes her. What would she say if she spoke to him? She doesn't try to explain that her moral compass has gone haywire, too, and she no longer knows what the truth its. She wishes fervently that she believed in horoscopes or tarot cards, like Helene. It would be a huge comfort to find something that would point to an answer.

Ginna snorts out loud when Sarah says, a little wistfully, that she envies Helene. "Helene," Ginna reminds her, "believes that someday soon we will all live in moon suits and recycle our own urine for drinking water. Please!"

On Thanksgiving morning, Ginna appears at Sarah's door with two pies. "Can I have Thanksgiving with you guys?"

"I thought you were working things out with Pat. What happened?"

"Just be glad you're not a Catholic." Ginna walks in and sets the pies gently on the kitchen counter. Pecan-caramel and cherry crumb, Zach's favorite. "This whole thing has been torture. First you see the priest, then there's Marriage Encounter, then individual counseling, and Confession, and Penance, and more counseling—and by then you really hate each other, but you decide to stay together just to get the Catholic bureaucracy off your back."

Sarah pours a mug of coffee and puts in front of Ginna. "So

where's Pat?"

"He's with his parents in Ohio, telling them what a failure I am as a wife, I'm sure. Leaving out the part where I had a miscarriage and he stopped talking to me."

"Didn't you say counseling was going pretty well?"

"It was, for me." Ginna sighs. "It's an incredible relief to finally talk about losing the baby. To acknowledge that something really terrible happened to us, you know? But Pat doesn't want to go to counseling anymore. He says it's like picking at an old scab, he doesn't see the point and it's only hurting us. He told me last night he thinks maybe he should move out for a while, take some time for himself." Ginna's eyes are scared. "That's code for I'm going to leave you, right?"

"He's not going to leave you," Sarah says reassuringly. "Come on, can you imagine Pat on his own? He can't even put away the orange juice."

Ginna stirs sugar into her coffee. "Do you have any Motown?"

"I think I have a greatest hits CD somewhere."

"Put it on. Pat hates when I play loud music, especially Motown."

When Row and Zach come downstairs a few minutes later, Gladys Knight & The Pips are singing "Heard It Through the Grapevine," and Sarah and Ginna are dancing in the living room. "No more turning down the volume!" Ginna yells, kicking one leg up in the air, Rockette-style.

"Yeah!" Zach runs over to join them and Sarah grabs his arms and wraps them around her waist. She reaches forward for Ginna and the three of them dance together in a line, snaking down the hall and around the dining room table, then back into the living room. Row stands watching them with an amused smile, too uptight to join them, Sarah knows, but privately loving the sight of his wife and son dancing in and out of the rooms of their house.

Row leaves a few hours later to pick up Hen, after Sarah and Ginna have hoisted the turkey into the oven, made cranberry sauce, and set the potatoes on to boil. Ginna is shredding carrots for a carrot-peanut-ginger salad when Hen arrives. Sarah manages to take her aside for a moment to explain that Ginna is here but Pat won't be joining them, that they are having marriage trouble.

"Oh, that's terrible." Hen looks crestfallen, as if it were her own romance gone sour. "What, is he cheating on her?"

"No, nothing like that," Sarah says quickly.

"Well what, then, is he a fairy?"

Sarah lets out a long breath in exasperation. She doesn't know how to explain what she knows to be true: that even a good marriage can falter, at any moment, for no apparent reason. She thinks guiltily of Row watching her dance this morning, the way he had tried to put his arms around her after she turned the music off, and she had slipped away to help Ginna in the kitchen.

They eat until they are stuffed and then carry plates of pie and mugs of coffee into the living room, where Row has built a comfortable fire. Hen is dozing in an armchair, and Sarah wraps a quilt around her legs. "Well don't we look like a Norman Rockwell painting," Ginna says with a big yawn, putting her feet up on the coffee table and stretching her toes in thick woolen socks.

"Except for the feet on the table," Sarah points out. "I don't think Rockwell would have approved of that—or eating with your fingers," she adds as Ginna dips two fingers into the whipped cream on top of her pie and puts an enormous glob into her mouth.

"Ah, then, screw Norman Rockwell. I always thought he was too sappy anyway."

"Actually, that's the one kind of painting I was good at," Sarah says. In art school she had been able to faithfully reproduce pretty domestic scenes by Rockwell or Kent, holiday tables and intimate kitchen settings with every detail in its place and contentment glowing on everyone's faces.

Row is watching football in the next room, Zach assembling a gigantic dinosaur jigsaw puzzle on the floor. Sarah watches them for a moment, then she climbs onto the sofa next to her husband and rests her head on his chest, his flannel shirt soft under her cheek. He turns to her, surprised. She listens to Row's steady breathing the way you bring a seashell up to your face at the beach, to find a rhythm that is both familiar and distant, to listen to something beyond the blood rushing in your own ears.

Stan

S tan hates watching the Macy's Thanksgiving Day parade. He had
to endure it every year when the girls were little—he even took
Sarah and Abby to 34th Street once to watch the huge parade balloons
being inflated. But now that his daughters are grown, he'll be damned
if he'll have the parade broadcast in his own living room.

Millie believes he must have been traumatized by a parade float
when he was a child. "Admit it, you're scared of Donald Duck," she
teases when he calls her on Thanksgiving morning. Lynda has run out
to the store for some last-minute shopping. If she suspects that Stan
still sneaks away, she doesn't show it.

Lynda has forgiven him for his "jaunt" to the Grand Canyon,
as he calls it, but things are not the same between them. He feels, from
the moment he awakens in their apartment to see the sun streaming in
through the blinds and his wife curled away from him on the other side
of the bed, like a chastened child. He has done wrong, and he must
now make things right again. Try as he might, however, Stan cannot
imagine how to make anything right.

Instead, he has begun to plan another adventure. While he sits
in his recliner in front of the television, a blanket thrown over his legs
and a book beside him that he probably should be reading, a road trip

is beginning to take shape in his mind. To the mountains of West Virginia. Coal mining country, where Stan made his first and perhaps his most lasting mark.

He had always planned to go back to Farmington, to re-visit the site of the 1968 mine disaster. Six years after the explosion, in fact, he had been on his way to West Virginia to arbitrate another coal mining case when Evelyn called to say that Sarah was in the emergency room. She had fallen from a horse during a riding lesson at Harmony Stables. Her leg was fractured in two places, and she had some minor bruises on her head.

Sarah was twelve when she broke her leg, and Abby was fifteen. Those were the years when Stan and Evie were happiest, when their entire household seemed to hum along effortlessly. Stan was putting in long hours working at his own law firm – the newly-minted partnership of Gershman & Rozin — and loving every minute of it. The cases were challenging, mainly workers' compensation, and he and Dick believed they were making a significant difference. Abby was playing cello and showing some real talent, enough to convince Stan and Evie to invest in daily lessons, and Sarah had taken up horseback riding. Evelyn finally relaxed, as if she was beginning to have faith that both girls were on track and would be OK, that their survival no longer required her constant vigilance. She always seemed so tense, in the early days.

And then Sarah fell from her horse, and everything unraveled again. Stan was at the office, his battered leather overnight bag packed for the trip to West Virginia, when Evie called.

"No." Stan found himself saying into the phone. "Evie, I've

got to make this trip. Can't you handle it?" It was a moment that Stan is not proud of. His wife did not manage small domestic crises well. Stan listened to her rage and cry at the other end of the phone and then slammed down the receiver and asked Dick to take the arbitration case for him.

He did not go immediately to the hospital. He sat in his empty office and fiddled with the papers on his desk, wishing fervently that his secretary was around so he could take her out for a drink, and then despising himself for the thought. Stan had never been unfaithful to his wife and did not believe he ever would be. But he was keenly aware that this night was the beginning of the end of his marriage, and he wanted desperately not to have to face that knowledge alone. He reached into a cabinet beside his desk and poured himself a small glass of expensive Scotch, swirled the amber liquid around and around in the glass, and then drank it down.

Stan can still conjure a clear image of Sarah in the hospital bed, the way she lit up when he came into the room, her face so small and her long hair sprayed against the white pillow. He can picture like it was yesterday the stretchy blue headband Sarah wore in her hair that entire year, its edges frayed from use. He never told her this, but the headband framed her face perfectly, pulling her long dark hair back so you could really look into her eyes. He was sorry to see the blue headband go when Sarah entered seventh grade and started letting her bangs droop long and low, till they almost covered her face. It was about that time that Sarah and Abby both stopped looking him in the eye when he talked to them. What is it about girls that age, Stan wondered, that they can't stand to have you look them full in the face?

And now—hanging up the phone with Millie, preparing himself to greet Lynda when she comes home from the store—Stan thinks he knows the answer. Over the years he has learned to look in the general direction of his wives—first Evelyn, and now Lynda—without actually making sustained eye contact. He believes, in fact, that he has perfected the art of gazing toward Lynda without actually looking at her full on, so as to avoid seeing the disappointment there. No sane person, he reasons, wants to truly see himself reflected in his family's eyes.

Sarah

Zach stands on the second floor landing wearing only his Captain Underpants pajama bottoms and a bright yellow towel tied around his neck for a cape, preparing to hurl himself down a flight of stairs. "Zachary, NO!" Sarah yells at the top of her lungs.

Row is shaking her awake, and she realizes that the panicked buzzing in her ears is the sound of her alarm clock. She turns to tell Row about her dream and finds that he has slipped away from her, his head tucked under a pillow. Nice. Sarah tends to believe that since her father is dying of cancer, Rowland should be available for extra comfort or conversation on demand. Her husband doesn't seem to share that opinion.

"Honey." She reaches over and tugs at his shoulder in a proprietary way that he hates. "We need to talk." Before a full-fledged argument can begin, however, the phone rings. The manager at Hen's building.

Hen slipped and fell in her bathroom last night. It was not a bad fall, the head nurse reassures Sarah soothingly when she meets with the nursing home staff a few hours later. Hen had banged her head and shoulder against the vanity in the bathroom, and there is a small fracture in her right arm, just above the elbow. She lay on the bathroom floor until eight o'clock in the morning, when Mrs. Shopes down the hall noticed that Hen hadn't shown up for breakfast. "I'm afraid, however, that she will require a higher level of care than we can provide for our assisted-living residents," the director of resident services explains, "So we are moving her temporarily upstairs to our nursing floor."

Sarah sighs and offers to spend the weekend with Hen, driving to Virginia early in the day on Saturday for a visit with Zach, and then returning by herself the following day. It's a relief to have a simple problem to focus on, one that she calculates will only require a Get Well card, flowers, and some sympathy.

Sarah and Zach carry a large basket of chrysanthemums and one of Ginna's French apple pies when they visit Hen on Saturday. They find her propped up in bed, one arm cradled in a soft sling that rests on her belly, a large bandage above her right eyelid where she struck the edge of the vanity.

"Are you wearing underwear?" Hen demands as soon as Sarah walks into the room.

"What?"

"I just read an article that says that modern women today are walking around without underpants on." Hen is brandishing an issue of *Cosmopolitan* magazine. Sarah raises her eyebrows and tips her head toward Zach, signaling that this isn't an appropriate topic of conversation in front of her son, but Hen is undeterred. "They think it's sexy, or something, but I'm here to tell you, it's unhygienic. You're just asking to get some kind of disease!"

"Don't worry," Sarah says weakly, leaning over to give Hen a kiss. "I'm wearing underwear."

"Me, too!" Zach shouts gleefully, delighted that the grownups are finally talking about something that interests him. "I have my Captain Underpants underpants on!"

Hen is distraught when Sarah arrives the next day, lying in bed with her hair uncharacteristically uncombed and refusing to eat. "Mrs. Levitsky down the hall came up to the 8th floor and we never heard from her again," Hen explains darkly when Sarah asks how she is feeling. "They send you here, that's it, kiddo. Say good-bye. Lights out."

"Mrs. Levitsky had a stroke," Sarah says kindly, reaching for a comb to straighten the fine hair that has clumped around Hen's ears. "You only had a very bad fall, and broke your elbow." Hen's bandage has been removed, and the bruise on her forehead is a shocking purplish yellow, making her appear battered and frail. Although she continues to grumble, she allows Sarah to gently comb out her hair, and closes her eyes eventually to nap.

Watching Hen doze in her hospital bed, Sarah experiences a familiar wave of peace and affection. She discovered long ago that she loves her family best when they are sleeping. The slow cadence of their breathing, its evenness and reliability, brings her such a rush of comfort that she sometimes keeps herself awake until Row has gone to bed, just so that she can enjoy the sensation. It is partly the comfort of knowing that everyone will go on breathing without her, that she is not required to act; and partly, she recognizes, it is the sheer pleasure of love without obligation, of being able to enjoy Row and Zach uninterrupted by their moods or desires.

She has not confessed this aloud since she shared it with the members of her new mothers' group, two months after Zachary was born. He was still not sleeping then for more than three hours without waking and wailing for a breast. She wished someone had warned her about this stage, which she later named Baby Boot Camp. Wished fervently that she could have prepared for the welter of emotions that accompanied her infant's sudden, insistent screaming in the middle of the night: outrage and love so intricately intertwined. When Zach was finally sated, when his mouth slipped free from her nipple and she could place him gently in his bassinet and, if she were lucky, tiptoe undetected from the room, she adored him without reservation. "He's so perfect when he's asleep," she had remarked to her mothers' group. "I just wish he were like that all the time." All four of the other mothers—whose children, she later learned, stayed asleep for five or six hours at a clip—had stared at her with expressions ranging from mild surprise to strong disapproval. She had never mentioned it to anyone again.

"Listen, Sarah," Hen's watery brown eyes are suddenly open and struggling to focus. She grabs Sarah's wrist and holds on tightly. "There are some things I want you to have."

"Hen. You're going to be fine," Sarah says. "The nurse said you'll be out of here in five or six weeks, as soon as the fracture heals and you can take care of yourself again."

"Oh, sure," Hen waves her good hand dismissively. "And I'm the Queen of Sheba. Now, listen to me. Downstairs, in my dresser, there's a big jewelry box. In the second drawer from the top. I want you to go and get it."

"Now?" Sarah lifts herself from the armchair. For the rest of the afternoon, she helps Hen to sort through a tangled heap of costume jewelry. There are imitation garnet and amber necklaces, strings of fake pearls, two bracelets hung with lacquered seashells from Atlantic City. Mingled with the costume jewelry are some beautiful pieces—a cameo brooch, a long strand of freshwater pearls, and a delicate gold ring with a single opal, Hen's birthstone. Hen presses the jewelry on Sarah and she takes it, planning to wear some of it and to give the rest to Maddie for dress-up. It is completely beyond her powers to tell Hen that nobody wants the things that she has treasured for more than seventy years. She wonders idly what will remain of her own life in another fifty or sixty years. *I'll go through all of my stuff before it gets to this,* she promises herself. *No boxes of jewelry and musty old-lady sweaters for Zach to pack up when I die.*

Sarah stands knee-deep in creek water, feeling the water tug at her legs, tightening her calf muscles to brace herself against the current. She is watching the water gather itself, mounting into frothy eddies around her knees, and then releasing to move forward. The shoreline has shifted since the last time she was here, the slim stretch of muddy sand now covered in a tangle of reeds and branches. This is what Sarah loves most about living near water: the sense of a boundary between land and liquid that is constantly in motion, that never presents the same face from one day to the next.

There is a remote beach near the Bay where Sarah has begun

building rock sculptures. Row and Ginna have never been here. It's likely that the owner of the beach, which sits on nearly fifty acres of marshland, has never noticed the presence of her sculptures, either. Sarah's stones balance on granite legs on the sandy creek bottom and rise up two feet above the rushing stream, fortresses guarding a swirling fluid metropolis.

Wallowing, that's what Roland thinks she is doing. Immersing herself in grief instead of moving on. Sarah pushes further out into the creek until she is standing nearly at the middle, icy water splashing up to her thighs, glad for her heavy rubber waders. She enjoys the shock of the cold water, the way it clears her mind. She has not spoken to Tom since she called things off after Kay's visit, and her longing for him is a physical ache. She scans the opposite shore until her eyes come to rest on a place where the land dips inward just enough to create a small, protected cove. She watches the path of the water for awhile, until she is sure: this is the place to begin her next piece.

Sarah returns to the cove three times in the next week, lifting and placing stones to create a sculpture that towers above the water, forming the beginnings of a curved wall with high stone spires. She doesn't know what it will look like in the end. But if someone asked her, she would say this: she is building a monument to the force of nature, to the relentless, unyielding power of this stream, to whatever it is that propels us out into deeper and deeper waters again and again, even though we are afraid and unsure of our footing, to haul stones heavier than our children up muddy, tangled riverbanks, to return home, cold and exhausted, and to wake up and begin it all again.

Stan

T̲he best way to play this shot," Hank Haney is saying smoothly into the camera, "is to make sure you never have to. It's one of the toughest shots in golf." He smiles an enormous white smile and swings his club, deftly pocketing the ball.

Stan has been watching golf on ESPN intently for five hours. He does not want to talk. He has barely looked at his daughter, who arrived for a visit this morning. There is a glint in his eye watching Hank Haney prepare himself for the toughest shot of his life, stick his butt out, rock back and forth from his left foot to his right, and take a swing. This time Hank misses. Stan shakes his head and slaps his knee in disgust.

Lynda decides this would be a good moment to plant herself in front of the television screen. "Sweetheart, do we have to watch this, really? We have company."

"Lynda, it's OK," Sarah says quietly. "I'm not company."

"Well, it's not OK with me!" Lynda's voice is unusually sharp and high-pitched. "Does the sound have to be up so loud?"

Stan glances up briefly and gives a shrug. Lynda rarely complains. He lowers the volume and she sighs noisily, walks back into the kitchen. Sarah follows her and Stan turns his attention back to the

TV while the two women bang cupboard doors open. He turns the volume back up.

He is aware that they are talking about him, aware of being the subject of much whispered discussion over the past several weeks. He tries to let their concern float past him, in the same way he allows his own fear to gather, shapeless, somewhere in the space above him, while he trains his energy on the things he can keep in tight focus: television. Sleep. Pills. His morning constitutional up and down the hall. Where he last saw his slippers. Pills. There is a pill for the fear—"anxiety," the doctors call it—but all it seems to do is to blunt the edges of Stan's terror so that it becomes a soft cloak, enveloping rather than stabbing him. Less alarming, really, and much easier to get comfortable with.

What is he supposed to do when the doctors announce they have "done all that they can?" Perhaps another man would gather his family together to hear his last words; or to tell them all how much he loves them. Stan can do neither of those things. Most days, he cannot bear to wake up next to Lynda; and then in just the next moment he is gripped by the fear of never waking up again. He knows that his daughters believe he is being selfish not to spend more time with them. And he knows, also, that it is utterly beyond him to share the black fury or the panic that engulfs him. Stan's one last, unheralded gift to his family will be this: to shield them from knowing just how terrified he is.

His wife and daughter come back into the room, Sarah holding a steaming cup of tea. Lynda reaches for her jacket, apparently going out, which Stan pretends not to notice.

"Go," Sarah says. "We'll be fine. Take your time."

Lynda nods and gives Sarah a quick hug. "The nail place I go to is just around the block," she calls down the hall. "It shouldn't take more than an hour."

The apartment is quiet with Lynda gone. Sarah reads on the sofa while Stan watches TV and begins to doze, the announcer's voice drifting in thick waves in and out of his consciousness. With Sarah nearby and Lynda taken care of he is, blessedly, at peace.

Stan is tired of people wanting things from him, giving him things, needing to talk. It exhausts him—Dick with the Parker pen, Sarah and her books, neighbors with their food. The Indian lady who lives down the hall brought over homemade potato samosas yesterday. Samosas! What Stan wouldn't give to be able to bite into a samosa, with its crispy, fried skin and spicy potato filling. It took all of his fortitude not to throw the plate of pastries in the kindly woman's face.

On the TV screen there is a Pepsi commercial: a grandfather traveling with a young boy, a few years older than Zach. "Grandpa?" the boy taps his grandfather's leg, bursting with questions. He wants to know how fast the train is going and whether he can have a Pepsi. They walk away together, the man laughing and rubbing his hand over his grandson's head. Stan clicks off the TV.

He is startled awake by the harsh, high wail of an ambulance siren somewhere on the street below them, and a few moments later, by the slam of a door as Lynda rushes into the apartment.

Stan catches the look on Lynda's face before she sees him and flees into the kitchen, covering her mouth with one hand. It is a look of pure dread, crumpled into relief, which he understands at once, and it pierces him. She saw an ambulance and thought it was coming for him. Without speaking, it is the one thing they have all agreed to protect each other from, the question, gathering behind their eyelids in the morning before they are fully awake: *what if today is the day?*

Stan gets to his feet and heads to the bathroom, glancing into the kitchen where Lynda stands with her back to him, facing the window. He should go to her. It's lucky that he can't speak, he thinks, because what he wants to do more than anything is to plant himself in the middle of the apartment and yell at his wife to stop, bellow at the top of his lungs that he's not dead yet. The doctors have explained that Stan has weeks, or maybe months to live. He doesn't know which to believe in, the medical experts or his own stubborn hold on life. *Just stop*, he wants to beg Lynda, *believe in me*! But Stan cannot yell anything at the top of his lungs anymore. Instead he continues to make his way slowly across the room, wincing in pain because his neck is bothering him today.

In the bathroom he bends painfully to lift the toilet seat, tries to take a piss and manages a dribble. With one hand, he feels around in his shirt pocket for one of his purple pills. He fumbles reaching for the water glass—damned fingers aren't working any more, the muscles twitch when he isn't looking—and the glass slips and shatters in the sink, sending shards flying everywhere. Damn it to hell.

Lynda rushes in and Stan sees in disgust that his hand is bleeding where a sliver of glass must have nicked him. Because one of the twelve daily pills that Stan takes thins his blood to prevent clots, he is bleeding profusely, soaking through the pink washcloth that Lynda presses against the cut. He lets his wife clean the cut and wrap gauze tightly around his hand to stop the flow of blood, the fury rising from his gut to his head and settling there, drumming beneath his eyes.

Sarah stands up when Stan comes back into the room and settles himself again in his chair. "Daddy? I could rub your neck for you."

Stan does not want anyone near him right now. He sighs and tries not to flinch visibly as Sarah places her hands on his shoulders, her fingers light on the bones that sit very close to the surface of his skin. She runs her thumbs smoothly along the grain of his neck and shoulder muscles, and after a few minutes, Stan relents and leans back against the pillows, letting his jaw relax and closing his eyes so that Sarah can't see his sudden tears. It is one of the rare moments when the black cloak lifts. When the world reveals itself to him again and Stan can take in, with one breath, all that hangs bright in the room around him, all that he wishes desperately to hold onto..

Sarah

For one year, in art school, Sarah dated a man who believed he could commune with the future. When something important was about to happen it would reach out and draw him insistently nearer, until he could see exactly what was going to occur, like a blurred photograph that gradually comes into sharper focus. When Sarah's friend Amy was eight months pregnant, Sarah and her boyfriend were on their way to see a movie and he stopped the car suddenly, and cocked his head at an odd angle like someone trying to catch a particularly sweet and unusual strain of music. "Amy just had her baby," he announced.

"No, she didn't," Sarah had said. "She's not due for another three and a half weeks." But she called Amy just to be sure, and reached her husband at the hospital, where Amy had just delivered a six-pound baby girl.

Sarah shivers now to think of being able to sense the future, to know its exact texture and the strength of its tug on the present. Isn't that what she thought she wanted? Someone, one of the nurses or doctors or social workers, to march up in a white coat, to take Sarah's hand and stretch it toward the days to come, the hospital visits and the late night phone calls and the inevitable end, until she could divine it all with her fingertips, like a message in Braille. Until there was no escaping it. No, thank you.

"What the hell do you want?" Row asks her. They are walking on the boardwalk after dinner, the Bay flat and shining under a grey sky. Sarah isn't sure how to answer, but she knows enough to say: More than this.

They talk all night long, until, sad and angry, they part in the morning. Row is sure that this is another phase Sarah is going through and that she will come running back to him. He throws his toothbrush and a change of clothes into a suitcase, and takes off in a huff for his office. Sarah watches him go, feeling numb and exhausted.

In the morning, she drops Zach at Ginna's house and returns to the creek. She works on her rock edifice all day, stopping only once to eat a sandwich. All day long and into the waning hours of the afternoon, she hauls rocks out into the water and places them, testing their position to be sure that each stone can withstand the force of the water cresting and swirling around it.

When Sarah sets the last stone in place it is already late afternoon. She unsnaps her waders and pauses for a moment on the bank of the creek, stamping her boots in the damp sand and stretching out her neck, then standing to watch the play of light across her stone towers. The sculpture she has constructed rises four feet above the surface of the water, higher than anything she has ever built before. In the late afternoon light, shadows dance in and out of dark, majestic pillars of stone that march from the shore out into the water, and then taper off, disappearing and re-appearing with the movements of the creek.

On a whim, she drives to Ginna's and picks up Zach, then swings by Tom's house and asks if Maddie can come with them for a walk on the Bay. Maddie is so happy to see her that Tom can do nothing but say yes, his eyes following Sarah as she pulls out of the driveway.

When they arrive at the site of Sarah's sculpture the sun has almost set, throwing rose-hued light against the stone towers. The children are entranced. "It's a city!" Zach cries, his small arms thrown open wide to take in the expanse of what his mother has set against the shoreline. "They're buildings, right, Mama? A whole entire city of them! If you were a fish…." He is crouching down now, knees on the sand, to view the structures from a different vantage point, "To a fish they would be giant, as big as the Empire State building!"

"It feels like a shrine," Maddie says quietly, reverently, standing next to Sarah. "We read about the Buddhist cave temples in school? They looked a lot like these."

Yes, Sarah thinks with enormous joy: Yes to both. She has built a city and a shrine. A temple to honor what human beings are able to create from the world that swirls around us, even as we are caught up in its relentless undertow. But also an homage to the force of that flow, to the beautiful and terrible power beyond our grasp. Sarah knows that she will come back here again and again, and that each time she will witness a different joining of water and stone, of light and shadow. She loves not being able to foresee every twist and turn in the water's path.

What she treasures is exactly what her husband would hate, Sarah realizes—the restless tosses and turns of the creek, its utter unpredictability. Oh, it might be possible to predict the water's route, and Sarah has no doubt that Rowland would jump to make that point, would launch into a dissertation on flow, force, and distance and how their exact relationships might be plotted over time. But what Sarah wants now, more than she has ever wanted anything, is to let go. To simply let the water move without charting it. To know it will follow whatever course it is going to follow, and that her sculptures will not halt the water in its path but will subtly alter it, creating new paths and eddies along the way.

A heron glides into view, beginning the evening's hunt for fish, and signaling to Sarah that it's time to return home.

Connie greets her with a thumping tail when she walks into her quiet house. Zach runs to his playroom, where she clicks on the TV to keep him busy. Row still hasn't returned. Sarah knows her husband will be back when his anger cools, after a day or two of sleeping at the office. She hopes she will know what to say to him by then. She feeds the dog, then opens the freezer and scans its contents, wondering what to heat up for dinner. Lasagna? Chicken Alfredo? On the wall next to the fridge the answering machine blinks, and Sarah thinks there are probably important messages to listen to. But right now she needs to stand under a hot, penetrating shower, to wash the chill and the salt of the Chesapeake Bay from her body. Everything else, she decides, can wait. She shuts the freezer door, pats Connie, and heads upstairs.

The answering machine light is still blinking two hours later when a call comes in from the hospital. Sarah runs for the phone and grabs it just in time to catch the liquid Ethiopian accent of Dani, her father's nurse. "I have been trying to call you! He is slipping in and out, Sari. It is not much longer."

Sarah looks at the kitchen clock and begins to calculate flight schedules, taking Zach to Ginna's, what to bring. She thinks her favorite pants are dirty, and wishes she had done laundry this morning.

"And Millie," Dani adds emphatically. "You are bringing Millie? Your father talks all day about how he is taking a trip with her."

Sarah's mom sounds like she is trying to disguise her impatience when Sarah calls. "Sweetie, are you still stuck on your dad and Millie? I told you, that's ancient history."

"But he said he saw her just last month." Sarah is confused, remembering her father in the café. "And he's been talking about going on a trip with her."

"Sarah." Her mother's voice is firm and kind this time. "That's just not possible. I'm pretty sure Millie moved to Canada to live with her daughter. She hasn't been around in years."

Stan

I f you want to know what the smell of death is, it's peppermint. Ask any hospice worker; peppermint is the fragrance of the room deodorizer sprays that are used to mask the odors of rot, blood and urine that suffuse bodies in their final states of decline. Sometimes tea tree oil or lavender will do, but to cover the strongest, most pervasive smells, peppermint is the only thing that rises to the task.

Stan stinks. His throat is pure rot, working its way from the inside of his body outward. Millie can still stand to be near him, bless her, or at least she has the grace to pretend. He knows he doesn't have much time left, and this trip may be his last. That knowledge makes him push on the gas pedal even harder. Millie has Billie Holliday playing on the car stereo, gives Stan a little smile as she hums along with Billie singing "It Had to Be You." Stan leans forward, straining to read the road sign ahead. Farmington, 18 miles.

He had plotted their route on the computer last night: southeast on route 78 until they reached Harrisburg, Pennsylvania, then east on interstate 68, which would take them across the southern Appalachian mountains and deep into coal country. He thought he might recognize these roads, but nothing looks familiar. He remembers narrow, two-lane roads winding through steep mountain ridges, but it seems that the road he drove on thirty-four years ago has been replaced by a state highway. There has already been snowfall up here; a thin crust of graying snow lines the highway on either side. Above them a huge billboard proclaims, "CONSOL Energy: Coal Makes America."

In Farmington, Millie points out a diner and Stan pulls over. They have been driving all night, and he is starved. He should be exhausted, too, he reflects as he wraps his hands around a mug of coffee for warmth, but all he can feel right now is the thrill of being here, returning to the one place where he once believed he was doing something that mattered.

Stan is stunned when the waitress remembers him. She is an older woman, in her sixties, with salt-and-pepper hair tucked back into a bun. When she comes to the table to take their order, Millie introduces Stan by name. "He's the lawyer who represented the miners' families in 1968," Millie says proudly.

The waitress puts down their menus. "Oh sweet Lord, you're that Washington DC lawyer. My brother Gerald was in Number 9 when it blew." She looks expectantly at Stan, and he suddenly has no idea what to say. "You and your partner—what was his name?"

Stan reaches for his notepad and answers, "Dick Rozin."

"That's right. Gershman and Rozin. You two are local heroes around here." The waitress, who introduces herself as Barb, looks flustered and sad, emotion crowding her face. Millie is the one who eases the moment, inviting Barb to sit down with them and tell her brother's story.

"Gerry was working the mines in the winter and going to school for his degree in forestry. He only had one more year at

Glenville State. Then he was going to quit the mines for good." Barb wipes the table slowly, absent-mindedly with her rag, then turns. "I've got to go tell Carl who's here." She points to a young man sitting at the counter. "That's Carl Meloski, the superintendent of Mine Number 20. His father died in Number 9."

Millie stares at the young man sitting across the room, who is devouring a hot roast beef sandwich with gravy and mashed potatoes. "How can he work in the mines that killed his father?"

"What are you going to do? The men here have to support their families." Barb's eyes are cooler when she turns back to Stan and Millie. "His father would be proud of him, becoming superintendent." She gathers their menus and stands up. "People who talk bad about the coal mines? Maybe they don't realize, around here, coal pays."

There is soon a cluster of men and women around their table, each one with a story to tell of a personal connection to the Farmington Mine disaster that had rocked this small town. Richard, a shuttle car operator and the father of two young sons who perished in the explosion. Sunny, wife of a man who had forty-five years in the mines and was killed just one month shy of his retirement. Ellie, sister of the woman who worked doing the books for Consolidated Coal. As they file past one by one to shake Stan's hand and express their gratitude, his own eyes are soon filling. When Carl offers him a tour of the mine, Stan doesn't have to think before he answers: he knows this is what he has come here to do.

Consolidated Coal Company's Number 9 mine was sealed shut for more than ten years following the 1968 explosion. The entrance to the mine's central tunnel is cut directly into a mountain, capped by an elegant archway of stone and brick that measures nearly 18 feet across. Stan feels only a twinge of apprehension following Carl into the gaping mouth of the tunnel, where the light from Carl's torch is quickly swallowed by the vast blackness around them. It's a good thing, Stan realizes, that Millie stayed behind with Barb at the diner.

Carl gives Stan a hard hat with a lamp attached, and a heavy jacket to guard against the cold. They board an elevator and descend quickly, plunging downward into a bottomless shaft carved into the earth. The light from their headlamps illuminates the glittering coal in the walls that surround them. Stan feels the cold in the back of his throat.

The elevator comes to a shuddering halt and Carl swings the door of the metal cage open. Stan follows him into a dark tunnel, illuminated only by the glow from Carl's headlamp. Carl stops and gestures to the shining veins of coal in the walls around them. "We're standing in the middle of a giant anthracite coal bed that's more than 900 miles long," he says, pride evident in his voice. "It stretches from Pennsylvania all the way down to Alabama. You're looking at some of the best, cleanest-burning coal in the world right here." They emerge into a large chamber with a moving conveyor belt, where a group of men are working with shovels, heaving enormous mounds of coal onto the belt. "From here the coal goes up to the processing plant, where it gets sorted and cleaned." Carl explains. The air is damp and cold and smells of soot. The men's faces are lined with grime, and they are sweating despite the cold, dank air. Stan can't fathom working an entire day down here, can't really imagine spending another hour with the press of dark, heavy earth all around him. "They work down here nine hours a day?"

Carl nods. "You get used to it."

Stan notices the ventilation grates that appear every few feet above their heads as they continue walking. He asks Carl about the ventilation system in the mines, how often it is inspected. The mine superintendent's face is serious as he explains what happens if the backup ventilation system fails. "Those fans stop, the men have 15 minutes to get up, max, or they're out of air."

Stan is wondering about the inspection schedule and the airflow rate, and whether federal mine safety laws are being adequately enforced. He has so many questions. He coughs and fumbles in his pocket for a handkerchief, wishing that Millie were here to take notes. When he gets back to New York, he'll call the office and get someone to research current mine safety regulations. It's obvious that his work here is not yet finished.

"Mr. Gershman." Carl has a hand on Stan's arm, and he is regarding him kindly. One of the miners has stepped forward and is clearing off a dusty bench. Stan stares at him, confused. He looks like Gerald, the waitress's brother, but that couldn't be. It must be the darkness, playing tricks on his eyes. It's so black down here, a man could completely lose his bearings. The walls press in around him, black and damp and breathing.

Gone Bolshevik

Stan has felt his life constricting, has watched the march of this illness with the numb horror of a bystander at a highway crash. Has looked on as the wide sweeping frame of his years narrowed sharply, telescoping down to one day, one hour, one spasm in his neck or one glob of blood in the bathroom sink this morning or yesterday. He can no longer tell the difference between one day and the next.

Now he looks into the faces of the miners and remembers what he had once known: that he is in the presence of greatness. He is surrounded by something far grander and more powerful than himself. Words are too timid for what he is seeing. He feels the majesty of the earthen cavern walls that rise up around them, hundreds of feet below the earth's surface where everyone else is walking, shopping at the Food Lion for dinner or stopping to tie a shoelace or open a car door or fix a sandwich, unaware of the sheer human energy thrumming beneath them. For a moment the cave chamber opens to Stan, expanding outward until it becomes a living thing, pulsing with veins of black.

A cough. One of the miners coughs, the walls have stopped breathing, and Stan is delivered back to the cold, dim air of the mine chamber. The man who looks like Gerald holds out an open thermos of coffee, inviting Stan to sit. "Why don't you stay awhile?"

Stan recognizes the coffee, and the moment, as an offering that he knows will not come again. He looks into Gerald's eyes and admires what he finds there—the flare of something tough and enduring. How had he forgotten this? The skill and determination that these men summon for their work, again and again, waking each morning with the grit and ache of yesterday etched into every muscle and stamping their feet into stiff, dusty boots to show up for another day. It knocks him over, their ability to forge something monumental from the raw depths of the earth. It reminds him of what Sarah does, transforming rocks into art. He sees that the miners are artists, too; and that they possess some strength in their core that Stan has perhaps shared one small part of.

Gathered around him in the dark earthen chamber, these men are his witnesses and he is theirs. Stan hears the beat of his own blood clattering loud as a freight train in his neck and ears. Reaching a hand out to Gerald, he accepts the metal cup of steaming coffee gratefully and sits down.

Acknowledgments

I am grateful for the remarkable support of many friends, especially Tracy Christiansen, Sonia Feigenbaum and Simone Schloss; Trish Moss-Vreeland, Carla Sinz and Bill Westerman; and Janet Mason, who is also a trusted reader. My family has cheered me on since I announced in second grade that I wanted to be a writer. Heartfelt thanks to Jackie Gilbert, Deborah Bottle, Fran Paris and Sylvia Johnson; and especially to Morgan and Andrew Bound, Summer Joy Banes, and Judah and Willow Bound.

My deepest thanks go to Jake, who inspires me every day; and to Bill, for the gift of being both embraced and free.

Much of this book was written at The Porches, where Trudy Hale provides a wonderful space for writing and retreat. I am also grateful for a generous grant from the Maryland Arts Council. Nancy Zafris contributed terrific insights on an earlier draft; and Debbi Wraga of Northshire Bookstore lent her creative eye to the final publication.

While this is a work of fiction, the Farmington Mine explosion was a very real tragedy. The Coal Mine Safety Act of 1969 brought a measure of protection and accountability to what continues to be a brutal occupation. Federal mine safety laws were passed in large part due to the vision and perseverance of Senators Harrison A. Williams, Jr. and Jacob K. Javits, assisted by an idealistic young labor lawyer, Eugene Mittelman.

About the author

Karen S. Mittelman is a Pushcart Prize nominee whose essays and poetry have appeared in *The Adirondack Review*, *The Comstock Review*, *Mothering* magazine, *Fireweed*, *Kerem: Creative Explorations in Judaism*, *Poetry Motel*, and other publications. An earlier version of this book received an award for literary fiction from the Maryland Writers' Association.